Werewolf versus Dragon

David Sinden Matthew Morgan Guy Macdonald

An Awfully Beastly Business

Werewolf versus Dragon

Illustrated by Jonny Duddle

SCHOLASTIC INC.

New York Toronto London Auckland
Sydney Mexico City New Delhi Hong Kong

Tonight,

look up at the moon.

Look at it closely.

Stare at it.

Now ask yourself:

Am I feeling brave?

Chapter 1

ULF WATCHED THE RADAR SCREEN. A GREEN line swept around it like the speeding hand of a clock. The radar bleeped twice as two green dots came into view.

"It's the dragons!" Ulf said to Dr. Fielding. "They're coming!"

Ulf and Dr. Fielding were in the observatory, the lookout room high above the rooftop of Farraway Hall.

Dr. Fielding was standing by a huge map on the wall. She had been tracking the flight of two dragons from their nesting grounds on the other side of the world.

"They've flown all the way from the Great Volcanoes," she said. She pointed to a red line drawn on the map, showing the dragons' migration route. "They're firebelly dragons. An adult female and her baby. They're about ten miles south and coming this way." Dr. Fielding carefully moved two red pins on the map, marking the dragons' location.

Ulf had never seen a dragon before. He looked out of the observatory window. It was night. Above the clouds the moon was nearly full. It cast a silvery light over the beast park, and down on the Great Grazing Grounds he could see lumbering shadows. The beasts were becoming agitated. They could sense the dragons too.

Ulf picked up a pair of binoculars and peered through them. Beyond the Dark Forest he could see the serpents writhing on the gorgon's head as it looked up at the sky. The spined armourpod was waving its trunk, and the long-necked giranha was peering from the top of its enclosure, snapping its jaws.

Orson the giant was standing on the bridge above the meat-eaters' enclosures, keeping watch over the beast park. In the moonlight he looked like a mighty rock, his huge shoulders silhouetted against the midnight sky.

From high above the clouds came a flash of fire. "Dr. Fielding, look!" Ulf called.

A moment later he saw another, bigger flash.

"That's the mother dragon," Dr. Fielding told him.

There was a rumbling sound in the sky.

The clouds turned red as the dragons flew nearer, over the Great Grazing Grounds and the Dark Forest. The sky was glowing with dragon fire.

Ulf held his breath. The rumbling grew louder.

Suddenly, two dark winged beasts emerged from the clouds.

Ulf looked up through the glass-domed ceiling of the observatory. "LOOK, DR. FIELDING!"

He could see the two huge dragons, their wings beating black against the night sky, their tails weaving like rudders, steering them through the air.

The mother dragon blocked out the moonlight, casting a black shadow down over Farraway Hall. She was flying beside her baby, sheltering it with her huge wing. She let out a series of short, high-pitched screeches.

"She's calling to it," Dr. Fielding said excitedly.

The baby dragon straightened its path, staying close to the mother, as both dragons flew overhead.

"Where are they going?" Ulf asked.

He saw two jets of fire, then a red glow as the dragons disappeared back behind the clouds.

"They're migrating to the Ice Mountains of Greenland," Dr. Fielding told him. "They won't stop until they get there."

Ulf looked out from the north window of the observatory, watching the dragon fire fade in the distance. He imagined the Ice Mountains of Greenland, far away in the wild, somewhere where beasts roamed free.

Ulf put his binoculars down and looked back at the radar. He could see the two green dots on the screen, bleeping further and further northward. "It must feel great to be wild like a dragon," he said.

Dr. Fielding opened a drawer and took out an old newspaper clipping. "Here, look at this. The mother dragon wasn't always wild."

She handed Ulf the newspaper clipping. On it a headline read: PROFESSOR FARRAWAY'S DRAGON. Underneath was a photograph of a man and a boy watching a small dragon taking off from a garden lawn.

"That's the mother dragon," Dr. Fielding said. "The one you just saw."

Ulf looked at the photograph, scratching his nose.

"That photograph was taken more than fifty years ago," Dr. Fielding explained. "The dragon was much younger then. She was born here. Professor Faraway hatched her from an egg."

Ulf looked up at Dr. Fielding. "Who's Professor Farraway?" he asked her.

"Professor Farraway died long ago. He was the world's first cryptozoologist, an expert on endangered beasts. Farraway Hall used to be his home."

She took the newspaper clipping from Ulf's hand and laid it on the table by the window. "Come on now, it's time you went to bed."

"Can't I stay up and watch the radar?" Ulf asked. He glanced back at the green dots on the radar screen.

"Don't worry. I'll keep an eye on them."

Dr. Fielding stroked Ulf's hair. "You need to get some sleep."

She bent down and opened a wooden hatch in the floor.

"Good night then," Ulf said, and he climbed through the hatch, heading down the long spiral stairs inside the observatory tower.

"Sleep tight," Dr. Fielding called.

At the bottom of the tower, Ulf opened the door and stepped out into the yard. He glanced across to the entrance gates in the courtyard, thinking what it must be like to live in the wild.

In the moonlight, the huge iron gates stood like silver wings. At their top were the metal letters: RSPCB.

The Royal Society for the Prevention of Cruelty to Beasts was Ulf's home. He had lived there all his life. It was a rescue center for rare and endangered beasts of every kind, from trolls to fairies, from sea serpents to demons.

Dr. Fielding, the RSPCB vet, had rescued Ulf when he was just one month old. She looked after all the beasts until they were ready to be released back into the wild.

Ulf glanced up to the observatory. Dr. Fielding was standing at the window watching him.

He turned away and walked toward the barns and concrete sheds: the feed store, kit room, hatching bay,

X-ray unit, and quarantine zone. Following a path out of the yard, he reached a small stone hut at the edge of the paddock. It had bars on the door and windows, and fresh straw on the floor. This was Ulf's den.

He stepped inside and lay on the straw in a patch of moonlight.

To look at him, curled up in his T-shirt and jeans, Ulf could easily be mistaken for a human boy. But if you looked closely, you'd notice his bare, hairy feet, the coarse hair above his eyes and on his cheeks, and the soft hairy palms of his hands.

Ulf was beast blood.

Each month, on the night of the full moon, he would undergo one of the great miracles of the beast world: a complete physical transformation from boy to wolf.

Ulf was a werewolf.

Chapter 2

TWENTY MILES NORTH OF FARRAWAY HALL, at the top of a rocky mountain, a figure stood in the moonlight.

His long fur coat was flapping in the wind, its high fur collar turned up, casting a shadow across the man's face. He wore a shiny silk handkerchief tied around his nose and mouth.

From inside his coat the man pulled out a telescope and looked up at the sky.

"Splendid. This will do nicely," he muttered.

The man glanced down the rocky slope. "Blud! Bone! Hurry up!" he called.

Two men were clambering up the mountainside.

The first, a small man in a ragged suit, skittered over the rocks like a rat, dabbing his runny nose with a soggy red rag. "We're coming, Baron," he answered.

"You're supposed to *wear* the handkerchief, Blud, not wipe your nose on it. We're incognito, remember?"

"Sorry, sir," the small man said, tying the snotty red rag around his face. He looked behind him.

"Come on, Bone!" he called down. "The Baron's waiting!"

Further down the mountain was a huge man with long greasy hair. He had a thick beard poking out from the handkerchief around his face. Slung over his shoulders were chains and nets. He was pulling on a rope, dragging a large wooden crate up the mountainside.

"Come on, you fat lump of lard!" the Baron called.

The Baron was standing at the top of the mountain with his hands on his hips. He lifted his foot, placing a pointed serpent-skin boot on the top of a rock. "How do I look?" he asked.

He ran his fingers through his hair.

The small man named Blud clambered to the top of the peak. "You look splendid, sir."

Blud sniffed, then lifted his handkerchief and spat in the dirt.

"Good," the Baron said. "I want to look my best on the night I send the RSPCB to their doom." He laughed behind his handkerchief, and it echoed around the mountainside.

"What are we going to do, sir?" the small man asked.

"We're going to get a dragon."

"A dragon, sir? How?"

"You'll see," the Baron told him.

The big man named Bone grunted as he heaved

the crate onto the top of the mountain. He lifted the front of his filthy vest to wipe the sweat from his forehead. "Where do you want this?" he said with a gasp.

"Put it there," the Baron told him, pointing to a piece of flat ground on the edge of the mountain. "Quickly."

Bone grumbled as he pushed the crate into position. "I'm going as fast as I can."

"Bone hates mountains," Blud said to the Baron.

"Stop complaining. Remember what you're here for!"

The Baron raised his right hand, holding it up to his side. His little finger was missing. "Now repeat after me: Death to the RSPCB!"

Blud and Bone looked at one another, then folded down their little fingers and held up their right hands. "Death to the RSCPB," they said.

"The RSPCB, you imbeciles!"

Blud and Bone sniggered.

Then the three men fell silent, looking up into the night.

A chill wind whipped at their faces.

In the distance, to the south, a burst of red lit up the sky.

"Quick! The dragons are coming!" the Baron shouted.

There came a thundering roar.

"Open the crate!"

Chapter 3

ULF WOKE LATE THE NEXT MORNING AND
found a note pushed through the bars of his den.

> *Gone on a rescue mission. Back soon.*
> *Dr. Fielding*

Ulf scrunched the note in his hand. In all his time
at the RSPCB he had never been allowed to go on
a rescue mission. He had never even been beyond
the perimeter fence.

He stepped out of his den. It was a clear, bright

day and the sun was shining above Farraway Hall, glinting on the windows.

"She left in a hurry," a little voice called.

From the paddock, Tiana the fairy came flying toward Ulf. A trail of sparkles was bursting in the air behind her. Tiana was Ulf's friend, and always had been since the day he'd first arrived at the RSPCB. She was a woodland fairy, the size of a dandelion, with clothes made from petals and stitched with spiders' silk.

"Did Dr. Fielding say where she was going?" Ulf asked.

"It was probably an emergency," Tiana said, hovering in front of him. "Orson went too."

Ulf headed up the path to the yard and looked in the feed store. There was a huge dent in the mound of grain where Orson the giant had slept, but he was nowhere to be seen.

"I told you," Tiana said, darting in the doorway.

Ulf went to wait for them to return. Tiana flew alongside him, humming to herself as they headed around the side of Farraway Hall.

On the rooftop a stone gargoyle turned to flesh and began stalking along the gutter, flapping his stubby little wings. "Poor little Fur Face," the gargoyle muttered. "Left behind again."

Druce the gargoyle had lived on the roof of Farraway Hall since the day it was built.

He leered down at Ulf, pulling a face as ugly as a clenched fist.

"Hello, Druce," Ulf said.

"Very pretty, Druce," Tiana said.

Druce flicked out his long yellow tongue, soaking the fairy in spit.

"Eeeyugh!" Tiana cried, wiping her hair. "Druce, you're revolting!"

"Blurgh!" The gargoyle blew a raspberry. He hugged his knees and rocked back and forth on his heels.

Ulf giggled, then headed across the courtyard to the entrance gates. He pressed his hairy face between the bars and looked up the driveway through the woods. "How come Orson's allowed to go?"

Tiana perched on Ulf's shoulder. "Orson's a giant. He can look after himself," she said.

"But I'm a werewolf," Ulf told her.

He listened, his ears twitching. He could hear thumping.

The treetops were moving in the distance.

"It's Orson!" Tiana said.

Ulf could see the giant pushing through the branches. Orson was as tall as the trees. His huge boots thumped on the ground as he came down the driveway. The sleeves on his shirt were rolled up, and he was wearing a pair of baggy pants made from a ship's sails.

"What have you rescued?" Ulf called as the giant approached the gates.

"It was too big to carry," Orson told him.

"Where's Dr. Fielding?" Tiana asked.

Orson pointed north above the trees. "Here she comes."

Ulf turned to see a black speck in the distance, coming through the sky toward Farraway Hall.

It was the RSPCB helicopter, the loud *thwock thwock thwock* of its blades cutting through the morning air.

As the helicopter came closer, Ulf saw a canvas cradle hanging beneath it, attached by a chain. He squinted. Hanging out of the cradle he could just make out two huge green wings and a long green tail.

"It's one of the dragons!" he said.

Orson stepped over the gates, and Ulf followed him to the yard. Ulf watched the cradle swinging as Orson guided the helicopter in.

The helicopter's engine was roaring, and the wind from its blades almost blew Tiana away. She perched on Ulf's shoulder and clung to his ear with her tiny hands.

When the cradle was directly overhead, the giant reached up and unhooked the chain from the bottom of the helicopter. He gently lowered the cradle into the yard. It fell open on the concrete, and the dragon's wings dropped flat by its sides.

Ulf stepped back. The dragon was enormous. He expected it to stand up and breathe fire, but it didn't move. Its neck was curled awkwardly, and its head flopped on the ground. The dragon's eyes were cloudy.

"What happened to it?" Ulf asked.

Orson looked down. "It was dead when we found it."

Ulf leaned forward and touched the dragon's side. Its scales felt hard and cold.

"Poor dragon," Tiana whispered into Ulf's ear.

Dr. Fielding landed the helicopter on the landing pad in the courtyard. Slowly the helicopter blades came to a stop. The yard fell silent. She came hurrying over, carrying her pilot's goggles in one hand and her medical bag in the other. "The dragons vanished off the radar after you'd gone to bed," she said to Ulf. "We found this one dead near Scartop Mountain."

"Where's the baby?" Ulf asked.

"This *is* the baby," Dr. Fielding explained. "There was no sign of the mother. Orson, would you mind taking it to the operating theater for me, please?"

Orson took hold of the dragon's tail and began dragging the huge beast across the yard.

"What are you going to do?" Ulf asked.

"I'm going to do an autopsy," Dr. Fielding said. "To find out how the dragon died. I'm going to have to open it up."

"Urgh! That sounds horrible," Tiana said. The fairy took off from Ulf's shoulder. "I'll be in the forest if you want me."

In a burst of sparkles she flew off over the feed store.

Ulf watched her go. As he turned back, Dr. Fielding was unlocking the doors of a large concrete building: the operating theater for large beasts.

He ran over to her. "Can I watch?" he asked.

Chapter 4

AUTOPSIES WERE AN ESSENTIAL PART OF crytozoology at the RSPCB. Though opening up a dead beast may sound horrible, it was also fascinating. Clues could be found about how the beast lived and died, and scientific discoveries could be made about the beast's inner workings.

Ulf watched as Dr. Fielding slid open the heavy doors of the operating theater. She flicked a switch and a huge light came on in the middle of the room. It lit up a large rectangular slab of metal surrounded by a shallow trench. This was the operating table for large beasts. Around the walls, shelves were loaded with tools for cutting and clamping, opening and probing.

Dr. Fielding washed her hands in the sink, then pulled on a pair of surgical gloves.

"Are you sure you want to watch, Ulf?" she asked. "It won't be very nice."

"Don't worry about me," Ulf said. He washed his hands and dried them on his T-shirt.

Orson ducked through the door, dragging the dragon by its tail. Hunched over, he heaved the dragon to the middle of the room onto the operating table.

The giant wiped his face with his shirt sleeve. "Dragons are heavy work," he said.

"Thanks, Orson," Dr. Fielding told him. She was loading a metal tray with surgical equipment: scalpels, scissors, pliers, clamps, and a crowbar.

"Good luck," Orson said. "I'll wait outside if you don't mind."

Orson ducked back out of the door into the yard.

Dr. Fielding laid a black plastic sheet beside the dragon and placed the surgical equipment on it. Then she unlocked the door of a large metal cupboard and lifted out a chainsaw.

"What's that for?" Ulf asked.

"A chainsaw is the best tool to break through a dragon's scales."

Ulf gulped. Then he heard a giggle.

Druce the gargoyle was hanging upside down, peering through the door of the operating theater. The gargoyle ran his finger from his neck to his stomach. "Bluuurgh!" His tongue unrolled and hit the floor. He dropped down from the doorway, sucked his tongue back into his mouth, and scuttled away.

Dr. Fielding laid a clipboard and a pen on the operating table and stepped down into the trench. "If you feel faint at any time, you must promise to tell me," she said.

Ulf picked up the clipboard. "I feel fine. I'll take notes."

On the clipboard was a piece of paper. Printed at its top was: *Autopsy Case Notes*. Underneath were boxes to be filled in: *Species, Vital Statistics, External Features, Internal Features, Cause of Death.*

"Species: firebelly dragon," Dr. Fielding said, walking around the trench. "Vital Statistics: male, about three years old. Approximately two tons in weight."

Ulf scribbled everything down.

Dr. Fielding pulled out a measuring tape and stretched it along the dragon. "Sixteen feet from head to tail," she said. "External Features: cuts and bruises to the left flank. Pass me the pliers, please, Ulf."

Ulf grabbed the metal pliers from beside the trench, and Dr. Fielding used them to probe a wound on the dragon's wing, pulling out a jagged length of wood. She held it up. It was as long as her arm.

"From a pine tree," she said.

"Is that what killed the dragon?" Ulf asked.

Dr. Fielding shook her head. "No. That's just a splinter to a dragon."

She felt along the dragon's side. "Some of its ribs feel broken," she said.

On the notes, Ulf wrote: *Broken ribs.*

"Do you think it crashed?" he asked.

"Possibly," Dr. Fielding said. "Though I've never heard of a dragon crashing before."

Ulf reached over, touching the dragon's wing. "What if it was struck by lightning?"

"Dragons' scales are fireproof, frostproof, and just-about-everything-else proof," Dr. Fielding told him. "Lightning can't hurt a dragon."

Dr. Fielding prised open the dragon's jaws. "Look at this, Ulf."

Ulf looked into the dragon's mouth and saw row upon row of razor-sharp teeth.

Dr. Fielding pointed to four large teeth at the back of the mouth. They had jagged edges and were blackened with soot.

"Those are the sparking teeth," she explained. "They strike together to light the dragon's fire. I have read about cases of dragons backfiring."

She shone a flashlight down the dragon's throat. "No signs of internal combustion here, though."

She closed the dragon's mouth and climbed onto the operating table.

"Orson," she called. "Can you help, please?"

Orson's face appeared in the doorway. "What's up?" he asked.

"Could you turn it over, please?"

The giant stooped inside and took hold of the dragon's wing. He heaved, rolling the dragon onto its back.

The wings fell outward. Its belly was covered in hard yellow scales.

In an area of soft flesh beneath the wing, Ulf saw a deep hole about a foot across.

"What's that?" he asked.

The hole was black around the outside and full of dried blood.

Dr. Fielding examined it.

"It's a wound," she said. "A bad one."

Ulf wrote: *Badly wounded*.

"Time for the internal examination," Dr. Fielding said, picking up the chainsaw. "Stand back!"

Ulf jumped out of the trench, and Orson quickly ducked back out of the door as Dr. Fielding climbed onto the dragon. She pulled the starting chord and the chainsaw roared.

Chapter 5

ULF STARED AS DR. FIELDING RAN THE
chainsaw blade down the underside of the dragon.

Sparks flew from its scales and a mist of dark red
blood sprayed Dr. Fielding's white coat.

She cut all the way down through the dragon's
belly. It opened like a zipper, and its guts spilled out.
Ulf had never seen anything so repulsive or incredible.

"What's that thing?" he shouted, pointing his
pen at a large green lump covered in a sticky
membrane.

"That's its stomach," Dr. Fielding said, turning
the chainsaw off.

"And what's that?" Ulf asked, touching what looked like a huge inflated bag.

"Its gas bag. That's where the dragon makes the hydrogen gas that it burns and breathes out as fire. We have to remove it. Any gas that hasn't burned could explode."

Dr. Fielding slid her hands underneath the dragon's gas bag and lifted it up slowly. The gas bag was full like a balloon. Two tubes were sticking out from it, one on either side. "These tubes connect the gas bag to the lungs. We need to cut them."

Ulf put down his clipboard and pen, and picked up a pair of scissors. "Can I do it?" he asked.

Dr. Fielding held the gas bag still as Ulf reached forward with the scissors.

"One tube is red and one is green. You have to cut the red tube first."

Both tubes were covered in blood. Ulf held the scissors over the tube that looked the reddest. He snipped.

"Now the other one."

He snipped the other tube, and the bag started hissing. "Is it okay?" Ulf asked, alarmed.

Quickly, Dr. Fielding handed him the gas bag. "Point it away from the dragon," she told him.

Ulf pointed the gas bag to the open doors.

Dr. Fielding leaped across the trench and fetched a box of matches from a shelf. She struck a match and held it up in front of the gas bag. "Now squeeze it!"

Ulf squeezed the gas bag, and a jet of flames shot out through the doors of the operating theater.

"Wow!" he said. "Dragon fire!"

Slowly the gas bag emptied, and the flames stopped.

Orson poked his head in. "Is everything all right?" he asked.

"Everything's fine," Dr. Fielding said, stepping over the trench, back onto the operating table.

Plunging her arms inside the dragon, she felt the stomach sack, pressing it with her fingertips.

The stomach wall was ripped.

"A rupture of some sort," she muttered to herself.

"Urgh! It stinks," Ulf said, getting a waft of the dragon's last meal.

Dr. Fielding reached into the stomach and pulled out a half-digested mountain lion.

"It didn't die of starvation, then," Ulf said. He was pinching his nose. He watched as Dr. Fielding picked up a metal crowbar from among the tools and began prising open the dragon's ribcage.

She climbed inside the chest cavity and checked the lungs. They looked like two enormous sponges. "Come see," she said.

Ulf stepped onto the operating table.

The top of each lung was colored bright red.

"Those colored patches are from screeching," Dr. Fielding explained. "This dragon was screeching when it died. It must have been in pain."

Ulf wrote on his notes: *Screeching*.

Next, Dr. Fielding reached for the dragon's heart.

She lifted it with both hands, and sticky blood oozed over her fingers. The heart had burst open. "Severe internal damage," she said.

Underneath the heart, Ulf saw something shiny and black. "What's that?" he asked. It looked like a ball.

Ulf put his hand in and touched it. It felt hard and cold.

"Lift it out," Dr. Fielding instructed, pulling the ruptured heart out of the way.

Ulf dug both hands in, trying to grip the object. It was perfectly round. His fingers were slipping.

"It's heavy," he said, trying to lift it. "*Very* heavy."

All at once, he heard a sucking sound, and then a squelch as the object loosened and came free.

Ulf lifted it out, staggering, then he dropped it on the metal slab.

"What is it?" he asked.

It rolled into the trench.

Dr. Fielding stared at it, and the dragon's heart

slipped out of her hands. "It's a cannonball," she said. "This dragon's been shot."

She walked around to the dragon's side and looked again at the wound beneath the wing. "Write this down, Ulf. Cause of Death: cannon fire."

Chapter 6

THE RSPCB HAD BEEN FOUNDED TO CARE FOR endangered beasts, beasts once thought to have been extinct. It had set up breeding and conservation programs, and provided medical care for sick or injured beasts, sheltering them from harm. Thanks to the RSPCB there were now laws against beast poaching, trading in beast furs, and beast experimentation. Cruelty to beasts had been made illegal. But there were still some people who were willing to break the law.

While Orson cleaned up in the operating theater, Ulf followed Dr. Fielding to her office. He stood in the doorway and watched as she reached for her phone and pressed the numbers on the keypad.

"Hello, can you put me through to the department for National and International Criminal Emergencies?" she said. "Yes, it is an emergency. A dragon has been killed."

Ulf was holding the clipboard with the Autopsy Case Notes. "Why would anyone want to shoot a dragon?" he asked.

Dr. Fielding was pacing up and down, holding the telephone to her ear. "Hello, it's Dr. Fielding from the RSPCB. Is that the department for National and International Criminal Emergencies?"

Ulf unclipped the Autopsy Case Notes and placed them on Dr. Fielding's desk.

"When will they be back?" Dr. Fielding asked. She raised her eyebrows. "Two days? But this is an emergency."

"What's wrong?" Ulf asked.

Dr. Fielding frowned. "Can I leave a message for an inspector?"

She looked up. "Give me one second, Ulf."

She changed the phone to her other ear.

"Yes. Can you say that it's Dr. Fielding from the RSPCB. A dragon has been killed."

She bit her fingernail and listened anxiously to the voice on the end of the line. "If you would, please, yes," she said.

Dr. Fielding put the phone down. "They're useless. All the inspectors are busy. Beasts aren't their top priority."

She sat down at her desk and turned on the computer. "Can you help, please, Ulf? Can you find the Helping Hand and start checking the archives for any criminals we have on file?"

Ulf walked into a storeroom at the back of Dr. Fielding's office. Filing cabinets ran along each side of the room. On top of them, stacked to the ceiling, were cardboard boxes and heaps of papers tied with string. The storeroom contained all the RSPCB's paperwork.

Ulf read the labels on the cabinets:

RSPCB MEMBERSHIP ... ENVIRONMENTAL SURVEYS ... BEAST POPULATIONS ... FOREST CONSERVATION ...

He put his fingers in his mouth and whistled. Something rustled in one of the boxes. Its top opened and a finger poked out. Ulf watched as three more fingers and a thumb emerged.

The Helping Hand crawled out of the box and scuttled onto a stack of papers. It tapped a finger impatiently, awaiting instructions.

Helping Hands are busy beasts. They run on their fingertips, and are perfectly suited to helping around an office, sorting and filing, fetching and typing.

"Dr. Fielding needs everything on dragons, criminals, and cannons," Ulf said.

The Helping Hand began rummaging through the files, opening each box and filing cabinet, pulling out sheets of paper, running its fingers over the words.

"The Helping Hand is on the case," Ulf said, walking back into Dr. Fielding's office.

Dr. Fielding was standing at the window. "Look, Ulf," she said. "Come and see this."

A shiny black car was coming down the driveway. It stopped at the entrance gates, and a man got out. Ulf and Dr. Fielding looked at one another, then hurried through the house and out of the front door.

"Can I help you?" Dr. Fielding called to the man as she walked across the courtyard.

The man was standing behind the gates. He was tall and thin, dressed in a long black coat, a black hat, and black leather gloves.

He tipped his hat, revealing black hair greased into a side parting. "Dr. Fielding, I presume?"

Ulf stood beside Dr. Fielding and watched as the man took a wallet from his coat pocket. He opened it, showing a photo of himself.

"My name is Inspector Black," he said. "From the

department of National and International Criminal Emergencies."

"NICE," Ulf read above the man's photograph.

"I've come about the dragon."

"That was fast," Dr. Fielding said, checking the man's identity card. "I was told that all the inspectors were busy."

"I was in the area. May I come in? We have much to discuss."

Dr. Fielding opened the entrance gates, and Inspector Black parked his car next to the RSPCB vehicles: a rescue truck, a Jeep, and four all-terrain vehicles.

He stepped out. His black shiny shoes scrunched on the gravel as he walked over to them.

He looked to the left. Then he looked to the right.

"Listen carefully," he said. "I'm currently in the middle of a top-secret investigation. The situation is extremely serious. There are rumors of a beast hunter operating in the area."

"A beast hunter?" Dr. Fielding asked. "Who?"

"This man hates beasts," the Inspector said. "We do not know his exact identity, but we believe he is in the area and in possession of a cannon."

"A cannon? *He* shot the dragon!" Ulf said.

The Inspector looked down at Ulf. "And who are you, young man?"

"This is Ulf," Dr. Fielding explained.

From his coat pocket, Inspector Black took out a notepad and pencil and started writing. "Is this boy a relation of yours?"

"Ulf is a werewolf."

The Inspector's pencil lead snapped. "A w–w–w–werewolf?"

"He lives here," Dr. Fielding added.

The Inspector's eye began twitching. He took a step back from Ulf. "Dr. Fielding, is there somewhere we can talk privately?" he asked.

"We can go to my office."

"I need you to tell me everything you know—

when and where you found this dragon."

Dr. Fielding turned to Ulf. "Ulf, could you give the troll its medicine and check the temperature of the incubator, please?"

"Now?" Ulf asked.

"Please, Ulf," Dr. Fielding said. "I won't be long."

Dr. Fielding took Inspector Black to her office, leaving Ulf on his own. He was thinking about the dragon. He imagined it screeching and falling from the sky.

He headed to the feed store, the largest building in the yard. Picking up a bag of frozen rats, he carried them to a large metal shed, the quarantine unit. He stopped at the big metal door.

Inside, a troll was thumping the walls. It had been suffering from a highly contagious case of cavern fever. Dr. Fielding had brought it in from Troll Crag to keep an eye on it.

Beside the door, she had left a bottle of antibiotic pills. Ulf pushed a pill into each of the rats' rears, then opened a hatch in the door. He saw the troll's green eyes in the shadows. It grunted, then stamped its foot and banged the walls. It didn't like the light. Quickly, Ulf threw the rats in and slid the hatch shut.

As he walked away, he heard loud thumping and chomping sounds. The troll was eating.

Ulf headed down the line of buildings, wondering what Inspector Black and Dr. Fielding were saying in her office.

He opened the door to the hatching bay, a square white shed two buildings along. On a table inside stood a fireproof glass incubation tank.

In the tank, two chicks were sitting on piles of hot ashes. Ulf could hear them chirping. They were newly born fiery phoenixes, just a day old.

When fiery phoenixes die, they burst into flames and burn away. From their ashes, their chicks are born.

Ulf checked the thermometer on the side of the incubator. Two hundred and nineteen degrees Fahrenheit. Just right.

He watched as a third pile of ashes glowed red hot and another phoenix chick burst into life. Three chicks out of four had hatched already. Dr. Fielding would be pleased.

Ulf stepped out of the hatching bay and looked across the yard. Dr. Fielding was coming out of Farraway Hall with Inspector Black.

"I must warn you, it is quite upsetting to see," Dr. Fielding was saying.

The Inspector smiled. "I see all sorts of things in this job," he replied.

Dr. Fielding opened the doors to the operating theater. The Inspector peered inside.

"It's been cut open!" he said. The Inspector turned away, holding his hand to his mouth.

"We had to do an autopsy," Dr. Fielding explained.

Inspector Black took a deep breath, then reached into his coat pocket for his notepad.

"What exactly is it that you do here?" he asked.

"I'm afraid I'm not too familiar with your work. Do you mind if I look around?"

"There's quite a lot to see," Dr. Fielding replied, looking at her watch.

Ulf ran to the Inspector. "I'll show you, if you like."

The Inspector's eye twitched. "He doesn't bite, does he, Dr. Fielding?"

Dr. Fielding smiled. "You'll be quite safe with Ulf. I'll be in my office if you need me."

She headed back inside. "Oh, Ulf, please could you check on the Roc and feed the jeepers creepers for me?" she called.

"Will do," Ulf replied. He led the Inspector to the vehicles in the courtyard. "It's much too big to see everything on foot."

The Inspector took his car keys from his pocket and walked toward his shiny black car. "I'll drive," he said. "There's a rug in the back you can sit on."

"We're not going by car," Ulf told him. He

pointed to the line of all-terrain vehicles in the vehicle bay. One was red, one black, one yellow, and one blue. "Have you ever ridden an ATV before?"

"Oh, I'm sure I can manage," the Inspector said. He tucked his trouser legs into his black socks and sat on the black ATV. "It can't be that difficult."

"Just copy me," Ulf told him.

Ulf got onto his favorite bike, the blue one.

"Shouldn't you put some shoes on?" the Inspector asked.

Ulf turned the key and kick-started the engine with his hairy foot. "Come on," he called, twisting the throttle and accelerating around the side of the house toward the paddock.

Ulf shouted "open" and the gate opened automatically. "The gates are voice activated," he called.

The Inspector wobbled as he rode behind Ulf. "Where are we going?" he asked.

"To the beast park!"

Chapter 7

ULF RODE OUT AHEAD, STANDING UP ON THE foot bars of his ATV, bouncing over the bumps in the paddock. Inspector Black rode behind, sitting carefully on his seat.

"How big is this place?" the Inspector called.

"Ten thousand acres," Ulf shouted. He pointed across the valley to the lake and the forest, then over to Sunset Mountain and the hills beyond. "Everything you can see!"

They sped past a bulltoxic, a long-haired bull-like beast that was chewing a bush of red berries.

"It only eats poisonous plants," Ulf shouted. "Its poo could melt your shoes."

Ulf looked back as the Inspector swerved to avoid a pile of green dung.

He rode on down to the freshwater lake. A crocoon slid into the water, and a rat fish jumped.

Ulf waited for the Inspector to catch up. "Here we have a wartolump," he said.

The Inspector stopped his bike.

In the shallows, a beast was snoozing, its fat, warty stomach rising and falling, and its thick lips flapping as it snored. It had two short tusks.

"It came from a lake where the water was polluted. Its tusks were rotting," Ulf said. "Dr. Fielding had to file them down. When they've grown back, it'll be released somewhere new."

Inspector Black took his notepad from his pocket. "And what's that one over there?" In the reeds, an ingo was wading, spearing fish with its tail.

"The ingo speared a broken bottle in a canal,"

Ulf explained. "It was spotted by the lockkeeper, and Dr. Fielding brought it in. She had to treat its tail. It needed thirty-six stitches."

Ulf revved his engine and sped off up the valley, heading toward a high-netted enclosure the size of an aircraft hangar. This was the aviary, where the winged beasts lived.

Ulf slowed down as he rode into a wire-mesh tunnel that ran through the aviary from one end to the other.

In the first section of the aviary, a beast with the head and wings of an eagle and the body of a lion took off from an oak tree. It flew toward Ulf and gripped the wire mesh with its claws, beating its wings.

"Is that a griffin?" the Inspector asked, riding alongside Ulf.

The griffin sneezed.

Ulf nodded. "It was brought in suffering from the flu," he said. The griffin took off and flew back to the tree, coughing.

In the next section, vampire owls were sleeping, perched in a row on a high wire.

"It's like a zoo here," the Inspector said.

"This is not a zoo at all," Ulf told him. "It's a rescue home. All the beasts are released back into the wild when they're ready."

The Inspector looked at Ulf's hairy feet. "What about you, werewolf? Are *you* going to be released?"

"One day," Ulf said, accelerating away through the mesh tunnel and out the end of the aviary.

Outside was a huge golden bird as big as a plane. This was the Roc. It was lying down with its beak on the ground. Its golden feathers had lost their shine and some had fallen out.

Inspector Black skidded to a halt. "That one's escaped," he said, seeing the huge beast out in the open.

"It's okay," Ulf told him. "We're trying to get it to fly away."

"Why? What happened to it?" the Inspector asked.

"It got blown off course in a storm," Ulf said. "Dr. Fielding says it's homesick."

Ulf pulled up beside the Roc's feeding trough. He dug his hands into the pile of beast feed and pulled out two meaty steaks.

"Come on," he said to the Roc. "They're tasty. You need to get strong."

He threw them high into the air. "Jump for them!" he called.

The steaks fell to the ground. The Roc sniffed one, then pushed it away with its beak.

"It doesn't look well at all," the Inspector said.

"Dr. Fielding's trying to make it better."

Ulf accelerated off along the track. Up ahead, nestled into the hillside, were four enormous transparent domes. He headed for them, slowing to let the Inspector alongside.

"Greenhouses?" Inspector Black asked.

"Biodomes," Ulf explained. "They're for the extreme-weather beasts. They're entirely self-regulating and temperature controled."

Each biodome was three hundred feet wide and one hundred fifty feet high.

Ulf stopped his bike. "Wait a second. Dr. Fielding asked me to feed the jeepers creepers."

The tropical biodome contained a thick jungle. Ulf pulled the lever on the side of the dome, and inside one section a hatch opened from the ground. Out rose half a cow on a spike.

Ulf watched as the vegetation started to move. Creeping vines slithered from the trees and crawled from the ground. Leaves parted to expose gaping green mouths. They squeezed and chomped and chewed the cow.

"Flesh-eating plants," Ulf said.

The Inspector's eye started twitching again.

Ulf hopped back on his bike and rode to the desert

dome. "In here we've got a sand whale," he called.

Up ahead was the snow dome. "And in there we've got frostbiters."

Ulf rode to the final biodome. It was shaking and flashing. Thunder and lightning were crashing inside. "The storm beasts!" he called.

"PARDON?" the Inspector shouted. "YOU'LL HAVE TO SPEAK UP. I CAN'T HEAR YOU."

"A FLOCK OF THUNDERLARKS AND TWO ELECTRODACTYLS!" Ulf shouted.

As the Inspector stopped his bike to note everything down, Ulf rode on, pointing west to a rocky hill dotted with caves.

"And that's Troll Crag up there," he called. "All the trolls live in caves and underground tunnels."

Inspector Black followed, holding his hat on.

"This way," Ulf called.

They turned down into a marsh, and a swarm of mosquitoes as big as crows rose from the ground and flew toward them.

"Hurry up!" Ulf said. "They can suck a pint of blood in five seconds."

Quickly, the Inspector twisted his ATV's throttle. Its wheels spun in the wet ground, spraying mud up his pants.

Ulf tried not to laugh as the Inspector's ATV lurched forward. They hurtled side by side down the track and bumped onto a wooden bridge. Ulf looked back. The giant mosquitoes were settling back onto the marsh.

Ulf and the Inspector crossed a stream to the foot of Sunset Mountain.

Inspector Black looked up. The mountain was pitted with black shadows moving upward, writhing between the rocks.

"They're rock-eating beasts," Ulf explained. "They're called kracks."

"What else is up there?"

"Listen," Ulf said.

Ulf and Inspector Black turned off their ATV

engines. From high above came a sound like tiny bells tinkling.

"Whistling mimis," Ulf said.

The Inspector wrote in his notepad.

"Why are you writing everything down?" Ulf asked.

The Inspector tapped his pencil to his nose. "I must make a note of every detail if I'm to catch this criminal."

"But what has any of this got to do with the dragon?"

"I'm dealing with a beast hunter," the Inspector replied. "To catch him, I must first get inside his mind. I must think like him. There are beasts here that, given the opportunity, he would love to get his hands on."

Ulf gulped.

"You mean he could come *here*?"

The Inspector closed his notepad and revved his engine loudly. "Right, what's next?"

Chapter 8

ULF ZOOMED OFF, FOLLOWING THE TRACK along the base of Sunset Mountain, down to a wide lagoon that led out to sea. "The sea beasts," he called.

On the far side of the lagoon, between the rocks, tall iron gates kept the sea beasts in. Running along the northwest shore were the marine facilities, deep-water docks, and the RSPCB speedboat and submersible.

Ulf pointed to a seven-headed hydra basking in the examination bay.

"The hydra was hit by a cruise liner," he explained. "When its eighth head grows back, we'll release it."

He sped along the side of the lagoon.

"Look! There's a razorjaw."

Just out from the shore, a baby razorjaw was jumping through the waves, following them. It looked like a thin red shark with spines along its back. As they watched it, a larger razorjaw burst out of the water.

"That's the mother. She was rescued from fishing nets. She gave birth here in the lagoon."

Inspector Black stopped his ATV and scribbled something in his notepad. "Interesting how the mother sticks so close to her baby," he said.

"She protects it," Ulf replied.

As they rode off again, the middle of the lagoon started to bubble and boil. A red flame flashed under the water. The Inspector's handlebars wobbled.

"Are you okay?" Ulf called.

The bubbling stopped.

"I thought the water just caught fire," the Inspector said.

"That's the flaming squid," Ulf explained. "It's

having its barnacles scraped. We've also got a petri-fied impossipus, two blind megamauls, and a pack of weed dogs. Sometimes we have mermaids, too."

They rode on past the end of the lagoon and then higher and higher up a hill.

At the top, they stopped and looked out over a vast moor. Beasts were roaming in fields separated by electric fences.

"This place is *enormous*," the Inspector said, amazed.

"These are the Great Grazing Grounds," Ulf told him, riding down the slope.

"Open," he called. A gate opened automatically, and they rode in.

An armorpod, a big beast with spines all over its body, rolled across the track, blocking their way.

"We'll have to go around it," Ulf said, steering in a wide arc, giving the armorpod plenty of room.

The Inspector stopped his ATV, beeping his horn. The armorpod snorted, and a long trunk emerged from the ball of spines. The trunk slowly stretched out and sniffed the Inspector. He jumped up onto his seat.

"Don't worry, it's a plant eater," Ulf said. "Big but friendly."

The armorpod sneezed, splattering the Inspector with sticky green mucus.

Ulf giggled, then twisted his ATV's throttle and rode out across the moor. "Come on," he called.

The Inspector followed as a bouncing boogle sprang down the hill. It had eyes all over its body and a long tail coiled beneath it like a spring. It leaped straight over the Inspector, letting out a squeak, then dived into a hole in the ground.

"What's that stink?" the Inspector asked, covering his nose with his handkerchief.

"Fear scent," Ulf said. "Boogles are incredibly nervous beasts."

Inspector Black rode from the stench as fast as he could, straight into a pool of slime. His ATV's wheels spun and he skidded to a stop. Up ahead, an

Emperor slug the size of a car was munching on the leaves of a tree. The Inspector stepped off his ATV, his shoes squelching in the slug's slime as he pushed his ATV free.

Halfway across the moor, Ulf was waiting. He pointed to what looked like a field of boulders and bushes. "Over there's a herd of tankons," he said.

Inspector Black pulled alongside.

"Where?" he asked. "I can't see anything."

"They camouflage themselves," Ulf explained. "Look closely."

The boulders and bushes were moving.

Ulf and the Inspector rode on. In other fields there were long-eared jackalopes, unga-bungas, and a duck-billed sphynx. Ahead, the track rose up onto a long metal bridge that ran above twelve high brick-walled pens. These were the meat eaters' enclosures.

"We have to watch out in the next bit," Ulf said.

Ulf and the Inspector rode up onto the bridge,

steering carefully. It had no sides to stop them falling off the edge.

The bridge clattered as they rode along it. They looked down on either side. Below, meat-eating beasts were growling and grunting, snorting and roaring.

"It's not a good idea to get too close, so we feed them from above," Ulf said.

A pack of demondogs was gnawing on a pile of bones. They looked up, snarling.

"I hope they're not hungry now," Inspector Black said.

A pigeon flew past, and the Inspector wobbled, nearly riding off the edge of the bridge.

"Mind the giranha!" Ulf called as a beast with the body of a giraffe and the head of a piranha stretched its long neck and snapped its jaws. It swallowed the pigeon, feathers and all.

"That was close!" Ulf said. "It could have eaten your head."

They rode along the narrow bridge as carefully as possible, over the gorgon's enclosure. The gorgon was climbing to the top of a tree, its hair a tangle of writhing serpents. They sped over a swirling black hole that was screeching and sucking in insects, then a feareater with eyes that burned red with fire.

At the end of the bridge they carefully rode down the other side.

Inspector Black was trembling.

Ulf switched his headlight on, lighting the way into the Dark Forest. He weaved between trees, jumping his ATV over tree roots and fallen branches. The Dark Forest was his favorite bit—it was where Tiana lived.

A stranglasnake dangled from a branch, hissing at the Inspector as he passed underneath. Inspector Black bumped along behind Ulf, glancing around nervously. From the trees came the sounds of forest beasts: hoots and squawks, howls and screeches.

In the shadows, Ulf could see the sparkles of fairies. "There have always been fairies in the forest," he explained.

"And there always will be," a little voice said.

Ulf looked up as Tiana flew from the trees and landed on his handlebars.

"What are you doing here?" she asked.

"I'm showing Inspector Black around the beast park," Ulf told her.

Ulf slowed down and looked back. The Inspector's hat had caught on a branch and he'd stopped to retrieve it. As the Inspector reached up to grab it, a tree crab pinched him on the nose.

Ulf and Tiana giggled.

Then, all of a sudden, the ground shook and they heard a trumpeting roar.

"You'd better get out of here," Tiana said, taking off into the air.

The Inspector was clutching his hat. "What was that noise?" he asked.

"That's the biganasty," Ulf said. "We don't want to get in its way."

Branches crunched and snapped as a beast crashed among the trees behind them. Ulf twisted back the throttle on his ATV.

"Come on, I'll show you a shortcut," Tiana said, flying ahead.

Ulf and the Inspector followed Tiana's sparkles down a long dark trail. They passed the swamp where the swamp monster lived. The black water was bubbling and swirling. They rode up steep banks and down deep hollows, the fairy whizzing ahead of them, guiding them through the Dark Forest.

At last they came out into the sunlight. Ahead of them, beyond the paddock and the freshwater lake, was Farraway Hall.

Ulf skidded to a halt. "Thanks, Tiana," he said.

"I'll see you later," the fairy replied, circling his ATV. "I'm off to collect primrose oil." She smiled at Ulf, then shot past the Inspector back into the forest.

The Inspector took out his notepad. "So fairies do exist," he said.

"Tiana's my friend," Ulf told him.

Ulf stood up on his foot bars. He rode around the lake, across the paddock, past the bulltoxic, and back toward Farraway Hall.

"Open," he called. The gate opened, and he rode into the yard.

"And that must be your giant," the Inspector said, pulling up behind.

Orson the giant was dragging the lifeless body of the dragon out of the operating theater toward the incinerator.

"That's Orson," Ulf explained. "He works here. He handles the larger beasts."

They rode around to the courtyard and parked the ATVs in the vehicle bay.

Dr. Fielding came out to meet them. "Did you see everything you needed to?" she asked the Inspector.

Inspector Black stepped off his ATV. His legs

were wobbling. Mud and mucus were dripping off his pants, and his hat was squashed.

"Most educational," he said. He took out a handkerchief and wiped the mucus from his coat sleeve.

Ulf started checking the Inspector's ATV for damage.

"Before I go, I have a couple of questions," Inspector Black said to Dr. Fielding. He opened his notepad and flicked through the pages. "Did you say you saw *two* dragons on the radar last night?"

Ulf listened.

"Yes," Dr. Fielding said to the Inspector. "A mother dragon and her baby."

"Dr. Fielding, if I wanted, let's imagine, to capture an adult dragon alive, how would you suggest I go about it?"

"You'd have to get it onto the ground first," Dr. Fielding said.

"And what would a mother dragon do if I shot its baby out of the sky?"

"She would follow it down."

The Inspector tapped his pencil on his notepad. "Then I put it to you that our beast hunter was not after the baby dragon at all, but was in fact after the mother. I believe he shot the baby so he could capture the mother dragon alive."

Ulf was looking up from beside the Inspector's ATV.

"Dr. Fielding, does the Ring of Horrors mean anything to you?" Inspector Black asked.

Dr. Fielding's eyes widened.

"I have heard rumors that our beast hunter is planning a Ring of Horrors, and so I suspect he has taken the mother dragon alive."

"But that's—"

"Rumors, Dr. Fielding, merely rumors at this stage. Though we ignore them at our peril."

Ulf stood up. "What's the Ring of Horrors?" he asked.

The Inspector looked Ulf in the eye. "It would curdle your blood if I told you."

He took a little knife from his coat pocket and sharpened his pencil.

"Dr. Fielding, I think we should speak alone," he said.

"Ulf, please will you take a crate upstairs for me?" Dr. Fielding asked.

"But—"

"Please, Ulf. It's in the kit room."

Ulf walked toward the yard, then peered back around the corner of the house, trying not to be seen.

"Dr. Fielding, we must find this criminal before it's too late," Inspector Black was saying. "I will search the crash site for clues. I suggest you step up security here."

"You don't think he would come here, do you?" Dr. Fielding asked.

"I suspect he may come for a fighting beast. From

what I see, you have plenty here for him to choose from. Perhaps your giant could make sure all the enclosures are secure."

"I'll see to it right away," Dr. Fielding said. "And I'll carry on checking the files. They may contain a clue to the beast hunter's identity."

"Good thinking," the Inspector said. "Keep me informed if you find anything. If he's as clever as I think he is, you could *all* be in trouble."

"What do you mean?"

"This person, whoever he may be, is clearly no common poacher, Dr. Fielding. *We are dealing with a master criminal.*"

The Inspector's shoes squelched as he walked to his car. His trouser legs were still tucked into his socks.

"Be on your guard!" he said, getting into his car. He started the engine, and Dr. Fielding opened the entrance gates. Inspector Black waved as he sped off up the driveway.

The huge iron gates clanged shut.

Chapter 9

"TWO LITTLE DRAGONS FLYING IN THE SKY. Baby goes BANG! Mummy goes bye-bye."

Druce the gargoyle was singing from the rooftop of Farraway Hall. His voice sounded croaky and out of tune.

Ulf glanced up. "That's a rotten song, Druce," he said.

The gargoyle gurgled, flapping his arms and wings. He looked up and sniffed the air. Black smoke was drifting in the sky, coming from the incinerator chimney.

"Bye-bye, dragon," Druce gurgled. His mouth

drooped sadly and he turned to stone.

Ulf turned away. He saw Orson's legs sticking out of the door of the feed store and ran to talk to him.

"Orson, what's the Ring of Horrors?" Ulf asked.

The giant was taking a nap. He was leaning against a mound of grain, snoring. Beside him was a half-empty barrel of apples. There's nothing a giant likes more than a belly full of apples and a little snooze after a morning's work.

Ulf heard Dr. Fielding's voice. "Calling Orson. Calling Orson. Orson, are you there?"

Orson's walkie-talkie was flashing on his belt.

Ulf unhooked it. "Hello, Dr. Fielding. It's Ulf here," he answered.

"Is Orson with you?" Dr. Fielding asked.

Ulf tugged the giant's ear. "Dr. Fielding wants you," he said.

"Mmm, lovely apples," the giant mumbled. Orson opened his eyes and stretched his huge arms. "That's better," he said, taking the walkie-talkie in his fingers.

"Orson, please can you secure all the enclosures and bring the biganasty in from the forest."

"Is there trouble?" Orson asked.

"It's just a precaution," Dr. Fielding said. "And remind Ulf to take a crate upstairs."

"Right you are," Orson replied.

"Over and out," Dr. Fielding said.

The walkie-talkie crackled, and Orson switched it off. "Better get back to work," he said, standing up. He ducked his head and stepped into the yard.

"Orson," Ulf called, following him to the kit room. "What's the Ring of Horrors?"

Ulf watched as Orson knelt by the kit room door.

The giant reached in and pulled out a thick rope. "Now, why would you want to know about a thing like that?" Orson asked.

"Inspector Black says the beast hunter is planning a Ring of Horrors."

Orson tied the rope into a lasso. He laid it on the ground. "The Ring of Horrors was banned before I was born," he said. "It's evil. Wild beasts are taken from their homes and chained up. They're thrown into a deep round pit—that's the ring. Then they're made to fight to the death."

Ulf was shaking. "That's horrible," he said.

The giant placed a huge hand around Ulf's shoulders. "It's humans that do it," Orson told him. "Not good humans like Dr. Fielding, but bad ones—rotten ones. Great crowds of them, gambling their money on which beast will kill the other."

"The Inspector says the beast hunter has taken the mother dragon alive," Ulf said.

"Then we'd better save her," Orson told him. "And when we do, I'll show the beast hunter the size of my fist."

He stood up and threw the lasso over his shoulder. Ulf felt glad that Orson was around. He watched as the giant headed through the gate into the paddock.

Orson turned. "Aren't you supposed to be taking a crate upstairs?" he called.

Ulf quickly stepped into the kit room. He grabbed a flashlight from a hook on the wall, then picked up a dusty old crate from the floor. It was full of junk. He carried it across the yard, heading toward the side door of Farraway Hall. In the flower garden at the back of the house he could see sparkles. "Tiana!" he called.

The fairy came flying over. "Where are you going?" she asked.

"I promised Dr. Fielding I'd take a crate upstairs," Ulf told her. "Come with me, will you?"

"No way," Tiana said. She started flying back to the garden.

"Please," Ulf called.

"It's creepy upstairs," she called back.

"But I need your help with something."

Tiana hovered in the air, thinking. "If I come with you, you have to go in first."

Ulf smiled. Tiana didn't like going upstairs. Upstairs was where the ghosts lived.

Chapter 10

DEEP IN THE WOODS, TWENTY MILES NORTH
of Farraway Hall, a tall crane was trundling through
the trees. It stopped and lowered a huge metal cage
to the ground. Draped over the top of the cage was
a tarpaulin sheet.

The small man named Blud stepped out of the
cabin of the crane. He slipped a gas mask over his face,
then reached up, pulling a gas cylinder from behind
his seat.

He lifted the corner of the tarpaulin sheet and
peered through the bars of the cage.

Inside, a huge dragon lay half conscious, smoke

drifting from its nostrils as it snorted noisily, in and out.

"You're an ugly beast," Blud whispered.

The dragon half opened its red eye.

"Want some more medicine?" Blud said.

He pointed a hose from the gas cylinder and sprayed the dragon's face with tranquilizer gas. The dragon's eyelid drooped.

"Sleep tight," Blud sniggered. He took the gas mask off and dabbed his runny nose with a soggy red rag. Then he walked out through the trees into a clearing.

In the middle of the clearing was a huge round pit. Blud walked to its edge and looked down. A tall ladder leaned against the wall of the pit. At the bottom, the big man with a thick beard and long greasy hair was digging. He was throwing up clods of earth with his shovel.

"Have you still not finished, Bone?" Blud asked.

Bone wiped his face with the front of his black

vest. "You can help me if you want," he called up.

Blud sat down, dangling his legs over the edge of the pit. "You're the digger, I'm the gas man," he said.

"I always get the heavy work," Bone muttered under his breath.

"If you've got any problems, then talk to the Baron."

Bone rested on his shovel. "Have you got the dragon?"

"It's sound asleep," Blud said. "I gave it a double dose. We don't want it waking up on us."

"The Baron said he wants it angry."

Blud sniggered. "When that dragon wakes up and finds out we've killed its baby, it'll be really annoyed."

Bone laughed. He pushed his foot on his shovel, chuckling as he dug deeper and deeper.

Chapter 11

FARRAWAY HALL WAS SET IN A REMOTE VALLEY on the coast. It was a country mansion, the former home of the Farraway family. For a hundred years it had been the headquarters of the RSPCB and the world center for the study of cryptozoology. On the ground floor, many rooms had been modernized, including the surgery, laboratory, and office. Upstairs, on the first and second floors, the older rooms had hardly changed in decades.

Ulf carried the crate up the back stairs and down the Gallery of Science, a wide corridor with drawings of beasts framed on the walls.

As Tiana flew alongside him, he told her what had happened that morning.

"But why would anyone kidnap a dragon?" Tiana asked, flying past a diagram of a sphinx's brain.

"Inspector Black says the beast hunter is planning a Ring of Horrors."

"What's a Ring of Horrors?" Tiana asked.

"Beast cruelty," Ulf told her. "Come on. We can check it out in the library."

Ulf headed past a picture of a mermaid's digestive system and another of the skeleton of a troll. At the end of the corridor he followed Tiana through the Room of Curiosities: a large room with wood-paneled walls. Cabinets and cupboards were crammed together. Tables were stacked with old objects and souvenirs. There were microscopes and veterinary tools, wooden chests and silver boxes. The room contained every artifact from the RSPCB's history since it had been founded a hundred years ago.

Hung on one wall was the net used in the first-ever fairy rescue and two wooden oars from an early expedition to study a South Pacific sea serpent.

Ulf wove his way between the cabinets as he carried the crate, and followed Tiana to a large wooden door at the end of the room.

"You go first, Ulf," Tiana said, hovering near the handle.

From behind the door, Ulf could hear moaning and groaning. The door led to the old library, the room where the ghosts lived.

Before Ulf could turn the handle, the door creaked open by itself.

Ulf glanced at Tiana, then carried the crate inside. The library was dark and gloomy. The curtains were drawn. He could just make out the bookshelves lining the walls and the two tall bookcases standing in the middle of the room. Between them was a large reading table. He could see row upon row of books, and more stacked in piles on the floor. The library contained every book ever written on cryptozoology.

"Fly along the shelves, Tiana. Look for anything on the Ring of Horrors," Ulf said.

Tiana shivered. She clung to Ulf's shoulder. "Look," she said, pointing up.

A shapeless glowing mist was moving along the upper reading level. Ulf heard the sound of footsteps. Then, as the mist disappeared into the wall, he heard a cry. A ball of green light flew out from a dark corner and shot across the room. Inside it, a mouth was screaming.

Tiana darted into the crate as the ball of light vanished behind a bookcase.

"I don't like ghosts," she said.

There had always been ghosts at Farraway Hall, and more had been brought in recently, rescued from houses that had been knocked down or grave-yards that had been built over.

The science of cryptozoology studied not only the corporeal or physical beasts, but also beasts from other dimensions, such as demons, angels, dream beasts, and ghosts. At the RSPCB, ghosts were treated no different from other beasts, and were given everything they needed to pass the time.

As Tiana flew to the bookshelves, Ulf placed the crate on the floor. He took the flashlight from his back pocket, flicked it on, and shone it around the room. Dusty paintings hung on the walls. He saw an old mantelpiece and a cracked mirror covered in cob-webs. In the corner of the room, an empty chair was rocking back and forth. It had been rocking back and forth for nearly a hundred years.

From the crate, Ulf took out a broken desk lamp. He placed it on a shelf by the rocking chair, then stepped back. The lamp began to flicker, on and off, on and off. "The ghosts like the lamp," he said to Tiana.

Tiana was flying along the shelves, glowing brightly in the gloom. She perched on an old grandfather clock. Its pendulum was swinging, tick tock, tick tock, tick tock. The clock's hands were moving backward.

"Why are they going the wrong way?" she asked.

"It's a ghost trying to turn back time."

Ghosts are restless beasts. They're made almost entirely of leftover emotions from unfinished lives, like fear or regret, love or longing. They exist only because something from their previous life remains unresolved.

Ulf could hear the sound of fingernails scratching down wood. He shone the flashlight on a cupboard in the corner. From the crate he took out a broken violin. He placed the violin inside the cupboard, then quickly shut the door. Music started playing inside.

"I can't find anything," Tiana said, perching on a stack of books.

"Keep looking. I'll be with you in a minute," Ulf said. He took out a porcelain vase and carried it to the mantelpiece. He was about to put it down when it flew out of his hands and smashed against the wall.

Tiana squeaked.

"Don't worry. It's just a poltergeist," Ulf said.

"No, Ulf. Look!" Tiana said, hovering by a low bookshelf.

Ulf shone his flashlight along the shelf, reading the book titles: *Handling Storm Beasts, Living with Zombies, The Spotters' Guide to Invisibles, Monsters of the Deep, The Dietary Habits of Vampires.*

"Here," Tiana said.

The Ring of Horrors.

Ulf pulled the book out and opened it. Inside were drawings of beasts fighting one another, with crowds of humans watching and cheering.

"That's evil," Tiana said, looking at a picture of a pack of demondogs attacking a dragon. "How can humans do such a thing?"

Ulf read to her: "The Ring of Horrors reached its height during the time of the Roman Empire. All kinds of beasts were made to fight to the death, the most popular being dragons, particularly firebellies."

"Stop," Tiana said. "That's enough."

She pushed the book shut.

"Firebellies," Ulf muttered. "The dragons on the radar were firebellies."

"It's horrible," Tiana said.

"If the mother dragon *has* been kidnapped, then—"

"I don't want to know."

Tiana was covering her ears.

Ulf imagined the mother dragon being thrown into a pit and made to fight.

Just then, he heard a scream. The screaming mouth flew out from behind a bookcase. Ulf looked over. High on a shelf, a book was edging out. Ulf shone his flashlight on it. The book was floating in midair. It drifted down in front of him.

He looked nervously at Tiana.

"Let's get out of here," Tiana said.

The book opened and its pages began flicking fast, as if they were being turned by invisible hands. It was a notebook, handwritten and full of drawings.

Suddenly, the pages stopped. Ulf and Tiana stared. The book was showing a picture of a dragon chick hatching from an egg. It was labeled: AZIZA THE FIREBELLY.

"Let's go. I don't like it in here," Tiana called, flying toward the door.

The book shut in a cloud of dust and fell to the floor. Ulf picked it up and put it back on the shelf. But as he edged toward the door, the book floated after him. It was pushing itself into his hand. Ulf felt a sudden rush of cold air as a ghost passed straight through him.

The door creaked open. Tiana flew out and he ran after her, shaking. The door slammed shut behind them.

"What was all that?" Tiana asked.

Ulf looked at the book in his hand.

On the cover of the book, written by a finger in the dust, were the words: *I KNOW WHO HAS HER.*

Chapter 12

CLUTCHING THE BOOK, ULF BOUNDED DOWN the back stairs with Tiana following him. They raced into the yard and along the edge of the paddock toward Ulf's den.

The sun was going down behind Sunset Mountain, and the light was fading. Suddenly they heard a trumpeting roar.

Ulf and Tiana both stopped.

"What was *that*?" Tiana asked.

Out in the paddock Ulf saw Orson pulling the biganasty on a thick rope. The biganasty was roaring, rearing onto its hind legs. Its three horned heads were gnashing as it bucked and thrashed. The spines along its back were sticking out like knives from its thick black fur. It crashed its clubbed tail to the ground, then snorted, scraping the dirt with its hoof.

"Come on, girl," Orson called. "Nice and easy does it."

"What's Orson doing?" Tiana asked.

"He's locking it up in case the beast hunter comes here," Ulf explained.

"Here?"

"It's just a precaution," Ulf told her.

The biganasty dug its hooves into the ground. With his massive arms, Orson heaved, and the biganasty slid across the mud. Orson dragged it to the safety of the Big Beast Barn.

"Is everything okay?" Ulf called.

Orson closed the barn doors on the biganasty and gave a thumbs-up. "Everything's locked up. The electric fences are on, and the alarms are set. I'll be keeping watch."

Ulf ran to his den.

Tiana followed him inside.

Ulf lay on his straw clutching the book. It was old and bound in soft black leather.

I know who has her, he read.

Ulf opened it excitedly:

The Book of Beasts
by Professor J. E. Farraway

He turned the page.

To whom it may concern.

My name is Professor Farraway. You have in your hands my most precious possession, my field notes from expeditions around the world, observing beasts in the wild. Inside you will discover things you could never have imagined—the secrets of beasts.

Use this knowledge well.

"Who's Professor Farraway?" Tiana asked.

"Professor Farraway was the world's first crypto-zoologist," Ulf said. He looked out through the bars of his den at Farraway Hall. It was nearly dark. The light was on in the observatory, and Dr. Fielding was standing at the window, peering through her binoculars. "He used to live here. He's dead now."

Ulf flicked through the pages. *The Book of Beasts* was Professor Farraway's very own notebook, full of diagrams and drawings, jottings and photographs. It contained sections on every kind of beast, from wartolumps to griffins, electrodactyls to jellystoats. Ulf saw photographs of a giranha, a phoenix, and a mermaid. He found a drawing of a troll digging a tunnel. In the margin was a note on how to hypnotize an eight-headed hydra using walnuts suspended on strings, and instructions on how to treat a fairy's sparkle.

"Look," Tiana said. She saw a picture of a golden Roc. The book said that golden Rocs live on the orchid mountains of Tanzania, and that orchid scent will revive a homesick Roc. "There are orchids in the forest!" Tiana said. "We can make the Roc better."

Ulf turned the pages, looking for the picture of the dragon.

"Wait," Tiana said, seeing a photograph of a stone gargoyle on a rooftop. "That's Druce!" The gargoyle was sticking his tongue out.

"Here we are," Ulf said, turning to the drawing of the dragon chick. "It opened on this page."

"Aziza the firebelly dragon," Tiana read.

"This is Professor Farraway's dragon. He hatched it from an egg."

"How do you know that?" Tiana asked.

"Dr. Fielding showed me a newspaper clipping in the observatory. That's the dragon that's been kidnapped."

Ulf closed the book. *I know who has her*, he read on the cover. He remembered the book being pushed into his hand in the library.

"He knows who's kidnapped the dragon."

"Who does?"

Ulf looked at Tiana. "Professor Farraway. I think he's a ghost."

Chapter 13

ULF HEARD A NOISE OUTSIDE HIS DEN. HE looked at Tiana. "Ssh," he whispered.

Ulf listened. "Who's there?"

He heard a stone fall to the ground and someone climbing onto the roof of his den.

Tiana put out her light and hid in the straw.

"Professurrrgggh Farrawurrrgggh," a croaky voice gurgled. At that moment, Druce the gargoyle appeared, his ugly face hanging upside down in the doorway. He smiled, tapping his nose. "What have you got there, Fur Face?"

Ulf pushed *The Book of Beasts* under the straw and stepped to the door.

"What are you doing here, Druce?"

The gargoyle vanished. Ulf heard him scuttling across the roof. Then everything went quiet.

"Where did he go?" Tiana asked. Druce's face appeared at the window. His long tongue flicked through the bars, darting under the straw. It coiled around the book.

"Hey, leave that alone!" Ulf said.

The gargoyle sucked his tongue in, pulling the book between the bars of the window.

"Give it back, Druce!"

Ulf ran outside as the gargoyle bounded away on his knuckles and feet.

Druce scurried to the yard and jumped onto the roof of the kit room.

"Give that book back!" Ulf called, running after him.

Tiana came flying past. "I'll get it," she said.

The gargoyle hopped from roof to roof over the yard buildings. He leaped onto the incinerator and sat on top of the chimney, gurgling in the moonlight.

"Professor's book!" Druce said. He started flicking through the pages.

Tiana flew up to Druce and pinched his nose. "Give it back," she said.

"Stop messing about, Druce!" Ulf called.

The gargoyle looked down the incinerator chimney.

"Poor Professor, dead and gone," he muttered. He looked back up. His face was black with soot.

Tiana stamped on his toe. "Now, Druce," she said.

Druce threw the book into the air, then bounded away across the yard buildings, muttering. The book hit the ground.

"Stupid gargoyle," Tiana called.

Ulf picked the book up. He wiped some soot off the cover, then clutched it with both hands. He watched as Druce scurried into the shadows, climbing

up the moonlit tower to the roof of the house.

The light in the observatory had gone out. The yard was dark and shadowy. Ulf glanced toward the courtyard. He could hear the scrunch of footsteps on gravel. In the darkness, he saw the silhouette of a man walking into the yard.

"Who's that?" Tiana asked.

"I don't know," Ulf whispered.

Tiana clung to Ulf's T-shirt. "What if it's the beast hunter?"

Ulf crouched behind a wheelbarrow.

The man turned on a flashlight and shone it at the door of the operating theater.

"What's he doing?" Tiana whispered.

The flashlight beam swung to the hatching bay, and the man walked over and rattled the door handle, then he walked to the quarantine unit and lifted the hatch. He shone his flashlight inside. Ulf heard the troll growl.

The man jumped back and walked across the

yard. He shone his flashlight toward the Big Beast Barn.

Ulf stood up to follow him, and knocked against the wheelbarrow. It scraped on the concrete.

The man swung his flashlight in Ulf's direction. Ulf ducked. He could feel his heart beating as the man crossed the yard toward him.

The man stopped at the wheelbarrow. He was standing directly over Ulf.

The flashlight shone in Ulf's eyes, blinding him.

Tiana flew up. "Who are you?" she asked.

Her sparkles lit up the man's face. The man's eye twitched.

"Inspector Black!" Ulf said. "What are you doing here?"

The Inspector pulled up the collar of his coat. "I'm on night patrol," he told them.

Ulf stood up, hiding *The Book of Beasts* behind his back.

"It's not safe for a werewolf to be out tonight

with the beast hunter at large," Inspector Black said. "You should be in bed."

He pointed his flashlight at Tiana. "You too."

"Come on, Ulf," Tiana said, flying away across the yard.

Ulf looked at the Inspector, then turned and hurried away with the book. At the corner of the kit room, he glanced over his shoulder. He could see the silhouette of Inspector Black walking around to the front of the house.

"Why is he snooping around here?" Ulf asked Tiana. "He's supposed to be out looking for the dragon."

Ulf could feel his fangs growing inside his gums.

"He's keeping an eye on things," Tiana said.

"He gives me the creeps," Ulf told her, heading toward his den.

Tiana flew after him. "Try to get some sleep," she said. "I'll see you in the morning."

"What about you? Will you be okay?"

"Of course I will. Fairies are safest in the forest at night."

"Good night, then," Ulf said, as Tiana flew off. He went into his den and closed the door tightly. Through the bars, he watched the fairy's sparkles shoot across the paddock toward the Dark Forest.

Down by the freshwater lake, Ulf could see Orson the giant. He was standing on the edge of the lake with his big boots beside him, dipping his toe in the water. He'd be up all night, keeping watch over the beasts.

Ulf lay down on his bed of straw. He opened *The Book of Beasts* and flicked through it to a page headed: *Werewolves*.

Werewolves belong to the beast-man family of beasts. They live in colonies and are similar in appearance to humans, but underneath the skin is a beast. On the night of a full moon they undergo one of the great miracles of the beast world, a complete physical transformation. The skeleton realigns from biped to quadruped, the hair and claws grow, and the teeth become fangs. With the first howl, the beast is unleashed.

I have seen werewolves leap into rivers and run fearlessly into fire. They will die to protect their own.

Do not trespass onto a werewolf's territory. Do not threaten his family. If you do, beware. Werewolves, in my opinion, are the bravest beasts of all.

Ulf looked out at the moon. It was nearly full. There was only one day to go until his transformation. He pulled the straw over him and tucked his knees up into his chest.

Chapter 14

THE NEXT MORNING, WHEN ULF WOKE, THE sun was already high in the sky. He could hear the sound of the Jeep. Dr. Fielding was driving back through the paddock from the beast park.

"Has something happened?" Ulf called, wiping the sleep from his eyes.

"Everything's fine. Orson's been guarding the beasts. Come inside, I've got something to show you."

Ulf hid *The Book of Beasts* under the straw and followed Dr. Fielding to her office.

"The Helping Hand has been busy," she said,

opening the door. On her table was a pile of papers, each with a name at the top and a photograph of a human.

"These are all the people we have on file who've been convicted of cruelty to beasts."

She picked the top piece of paper from the pile and handed it to Ulf. On it he saw a photograph of a man with a tall white hat and a thin mustache. *Franco Ravioli, chef. Caught serving impossipus tentacles in his restaurant.*

On the sheet below he saw a photograph of a woman with red lipstick and a diamond necklace. *Lucretia Da Silva, boutique manageress. Caught selling jackalope-fur coats.*

On the next sheet was a photograph of a fat man with a bald head. *Billy Buck, factory owner. Caught dumping chemical waste in Farleigh swamp, polluting a crocoon habitat.*

"None of them sound like hunters," Ulf said.

"Criminals tend to flock together," Dr. Fielding

told him. "These should give us a lead to finding the beast hunter."

Just then, the telephone rang.

Dr. Fielding picked up the handset. "Hello, RSPCB."

Ulf thumbed through the pile of papers. There were over a hundred criminals.

"Yes, I've got some names to give you," he heard Dr. Fielding say. She picked up a rubber band, then glanced out of the window. "Yes, Orson's here. He's been keeping watch. No one gets past Orson."

She winked at Ulf. Then she wedged the handset between her chin and her shoulder, and stretched the rubber band around the pile of papers. "Yes, yes," she said. "Ulf is looking a bit tired now you mention it."

Dr. Fielding smiled. "Okay. See you in half an hour." She put the phone down.

"Who was that?" Ulf asked.

"Inspector Black. He says he's got some news."

"Has he found the dragon?"

"He's coming over."

Dr. Fielding stood up. "Well, I'd better get on with my work now, Ulf."

Ulf opened the door to leave. As he did so, from upstairs he heard moanings and groanings. He listened. The ghosts sounded restless.

"Dr. Fielding, can I ask you a question?" he said, turning back to her.

"Of course you can, Ulf."

"Is Professor Farraway a ghost?"

Dr. Fielding looked at Ulf strangely. "Professor Farraway? Why would you think that?"

"He's dead, isn't he?" Ulf asked.

"Not everyone becomes a ghost, Ulf," she said. "Ghosts only come from unfinished lives."

Ulf glanced up the stairs. "What was Professor Farraway like?" he asked.

"I never knew him but I understand that he was a kind man," Dr. Fielding said. "When he died, he left his entire fortune to fund the RSPCB."

"I think he knows who's got the dragon," Ulf said.

Dr. Fielding looked out of the door as the groaning noises grew louder. "What on earth's the matter upstairs?" she asked.

"I'll go and see," Ulf said.

He ran up the back stairs two at a time. He raced along the Gallery of Science and through the Room of Curiosities, his hairy feet skidding to a stop outside the library door.

The door creaked open, and the sound of moaning and groaning stopped. Ulf peered into the gloomy room. He took a deep breath and stepped inside. An icy draft swept through him, and the door slammed shut.

Ulf stood listening in the darkness. He could hear the rocking chair rocking on the floorboards. From up high came the sound of footsteps.

Ulf walked through the room, feeling his way around the bookcases.

"Professor Farraway?" he whispered. "Are you in here?"

As he spoke, in the gloom, a candle flickered on, the flame lighting by itself. It lit up a large painting on the wall. Ulf walked toward it.

It was a painting of an old man wearing a tweed suit, sitting at a writing desk. His hair was gray and thin, and he was looking up from his notebook. His eyes were smiling. Underneath, a gold nameplate read:

LORD JOHN EVERARD FARRAWAY

PROFESSOR OF CRYPTOZOOLOGY

Ulf shivered, feeling the hairs on his neck and back standing on end.

"Professor?"

The candle flickered. It was standing on a little table. The table started shaking.

"Who has the dragon?" Ulf asked.

On the table, a line appeared in the dust. An

Lord John Everard Farraway
Professor of Cryptozoology

invisible finger was sliding over the wood, writing the letter *M*.

Ulf watched: *A . . . R*.

Letter by letter, a word appeared in the dust. *MARACKAI*.

Ulf looked up at the picture. "Marackai? Who's Marackai?" he asked.

An icy draft swept through him, and the candle blew out.

From outside, Ulf heard the sound of a truck pulling up in the courtyard. He raced out of the library and bounded downstairs and out through the front door.

Dr. Fielding was standing by a huge black truck. Inspector Black was back. The driver's door opened, and the Inspector jumped down.

"Dr. Fielding! Quick, Dr. Fielding!" Ulf called.

"Bad news, Ulf," Dr. Fielding said, as he ran over. "The Inspector's found a pit in Furnace Woods. The rumors about the Ring of Horrors are true."

"I know who's got the dragon!" Ulf said.

"Dr. Fielding, do you have that list of criminals?" the Inspector asked.

"It's Marackai!" Ulf said. "His name's Marackai!"

The Inspector looked at Ulf, his eye twitching. "What did you say?"

"Marackai! Marackai's got the dragon! I saw it in the library. Marackai was written in the dust."

"Pardon, Ulf?" Dr. Fielding said, looking confused.

"Does the werewolf always act so peculiarly?" Inspector Black asked. "Or is there a full moon tonight?"

Dr. Fielding pressed her hand to Ulf's forehead. "You are starting to get hot, Ulf," she told him. "Your wolf brain must be activating."

"But it's true, Dr. Fielding. His name's Marackai."

"I'll check to see if it's in the files," Dr. Fielding said. "I promise."

Inspector Black put his hand on Dr. Fielding's shoulder and started walking her away toward the house. "Try to keep the werewolf from interfering," he whispered. "We can't afford to get sidetracked."

"Marackai . . . Now where do I know that name from?" Dr. Fielding said, opening the front door.

"Isn't it a place in Africa?" the Inspector asked.

Ulf watched as Dr. Fielding and Inspector Black walked inside. The front door closed behind them.

Chapter 15

ULF CREPT ACROSS THE COURTYARD AND crouched in the flower bed outside Dr. Fielding's office. He peered in through the window and saw Inspector Black talking.

"Are you snooping?" a little voice asked.

Ulf looked down. Tiana was sitting on a flower.

"Professor Farraway *is* a ghost," he whispered to her. "He knows who's got the dragon—it's Marackai."

"Marackai?" Tiana asked. "Who's Marackai?"

"That's what we've got to find out," Ulf said.

Ulf and Tiana looked through the window. Inspector Black was sitting on the corner of Dr.

Fielding's desk, leafing through the pile of papers with the names and photos of the criminals.

"This will be very useful," the Inspector said, smiling at Dr. Fielding. "I shall check out each and every one."

The Inspector tapped the papers on the desk, straightening the pile, then put a rubber band around them.

"One more thing, Dr. Fielding," he said. "May I borrow the giant? I should like to take him to Furnace Woods."

"Orson?" Dr. Fielding asked. "Why do you need Orson?"

"I understand Mr. Orson can handle any large beast. If there's a dragon that needs rescuing, I may need his expertise."

"I'll come too," she said.

"No, Dr. Fielding. You must stay here and keep watch over the beast park," Inspector Black told her. He looked left and then right. "The RSPCB must be guarded at all times. This criminal may still be after another fighting beast."

"He's taking Orson," Ulf whispered to Tiana.

The Inspector straightened his hat and turned the collar up on his coat. "Well, there's no time to lose. We must act now."

"Quick, he's leaving!" Ulf said.

Ulf and Tiana raced around into the yard as Inspector Black and Dr. Fielding came out of the side door of the house.

"Giant, we will need ropes, chains, and apples!" the Inspector called. Orson was leaning on the roof of the kit room, watching over the beast park.

"Apples?" Orson asked. "Did you say apples?"

"Lots of apples!" the Inspector told him.

"Orson, the Inspector needs you to go with him to Furnace Woods," Dr. Fielding explained, walking across to the giant. "He's located the Ring of Horrors."

"I'll open the truck," Inspector Black said, striding past Ulf into the courtyard.

Orson helped Dr. Fielding carry ropes and chains from the kit room. On the end of one of the chains was a huge padlock. Orson slung them over his back. Then he ducked into the feed store and fetched two barrels full of apples, holding one in each hand.

Ulf ran over to the giant. "Why is the Inspector taking apples?" Ulf asked.

"Apples are tasty," Orson said.

They loaded everything into the back of the truck.

"In you go, too, Mr. Orson," the Inspector said.

"In the truck? But I usually walk," Orson told him.

"There's no time for that. In you get."

Awkwardly, Orson stepped up and squeezed himself into the back of the truck. He had to bend over with his knees tucked against his chest.

Ulf looked at him hunched up inside. "Do you want me to come too?" he asked.

"You must stay here, werewolf," the Inspector said.

Orson winked. "Thanks, Ulf, but I'll be fine. Keep an eye on things here for me."

"We will," Tiana replied, hovering by Ulf's side.

"There's no time to chat," Inspector Black said, shooing the fairy out of the way with his gloved hand. "We're in a hurry." He pushed past Ulf and slammed the back doors of the truck.

The Inspector climbed up into the front seat as Dr. Fielding opened the entrance gates. He revved the engine, and the truck's wheels scrunched on the gravel.

Ulf saw Tiana lying on the ground. "Are you okay?" he asked, picking her up.

Sparkles fizzed weakly from her wings. She lay crumpled on Ulf's hand as the truck drove off up the driveway.

"He hit me," Tiana said. "Inspector Black hit me."

Chapter 16

DR. FIELDING CLOSED THE ENTRANCE GATES. "Come on, Ulf, it's time for your checkup," she told him.

"There's something wrong with Tiana," Ulf said. He held out his hand to show Dr. Fielding. The little fairy was gripping on to the hairs on Ulf's palm, trying not to topple. She looked pale.

Dr. Fielding knelt down. "What happened to you, Tiana?" she asked.

"I got bashed," Tiana said.

"Inspector Black hit her," Ulf explained.

"I'm sure he didn't mean to," Dr. Fielding said.

She checked the fairy's wing. It was bent and crumpled like tissue paper. "It's not broken but you've lost your sparkle, Tiana. No flying for a while. Come on, Ulf. We'll get her comfortable."

Ulf carried Tiana inside. He followed Dr. Fielding into her surgery, the room where she performed health checks and smaller operations.

Dr. Fielding placed Tiana on a ball of cotton wool. "You'll be okay there, Tiana," she said. "You need to rest."

Tiana lay down and closed her eyes.

"Right, now let's have a look at you, Ulf," Dr. Fielding said.

Every month, on the day of his transformation, Dr. Fielding gave Ulf a full physical examination to monitor his development. The RSPCB kept records of all of their beasts, gathering as much scientific information as they could before the beasts were released back into the wild. Werewolves were no exception.

Ulf sat on the edge of the examination table.

"Did you get any sleep last night?" Dr. Fielding asked him, flicking through his medical records.

"Not much," Ulf replied.

"You're turning nocturnal," Dr. Fielding told him. "How are you feeling?"

"I feel strong. I could have gone with Orson."

"It isn't safe for you, I'm afraid," Dr. Fielding said.

"But I'm a werewolf. I'm not scared."

"I need you here, Ulf, to help me guard the beasts."

Dr. Fielding held his hand and pressed her fingers on his wrist, checking his pulse. She looked at her watch and counted.

"It's racing," she said. "Two hundred and twenty beats per minute."

"Is that good?" Ulf asked.

"For a werewolf it is."

Ulf opened his mouth, and Dr. Fielding looked inside.

"The tips of your fangs are coming through your gums," she said.

Ulf's jaw and tongue were getting longer. Dr. Fielding took a thermometer from her coat pocket. She popped it into Ulf's mouth.

"Hold that there," she said.

As Ulf rolled the thermometer with his tongue, Dr. Fielding picked up his medical records and began making notes.

"But what if Orson needs help?" Ulf asked, trying not to spit the thermometer out.

"Orson will be fine. You must look after yourself. It's only a few hours until your transformation."

She took the thermometer from Ulf's mouth and looked at it, checking the temperature. "Your blood is warming up," she said. "One hundred seventeen degrees." She wiped the thermometer and placed it on the counter. "Now, let's have a look at your skin."

Ulf pulled off his T-shirt, and Dr. Fielding examined his back and chest.

"The hair is beginning to sprout," she said. "Your shoulders and chest are getting bigger."

Ulf's skeleton was beginning to realign.

He stood against the wall, and Dr. Fielding measured his height.

"You're almost an inch taller than normal," she said.

From a metal shelf, she handed Ulf the pressure ball, a black rubber ball with a tube connected to a pressure gauge. Ulf squeezed the ball, and the dial on the gauge swung to the red zone.

"Good," Dr. Fielding said. "Your muscles are strengthening."

She pointed to the eye chart on the far wall. "Now read me the last line."

The letters were tiny.

"J V R Q P L B," Ulf read clearly.

"Perfect vision," Dr. Fielding said. "Your senses are sharpening. You can go up to the observatory and keep watch over the beast park. We'll need your eyes now that Orson's not here."

"Can I go too?" a little voice asked. Tiana was sitting up on the ball of cotton wool.

"Ulf, will you look after Tiana?" Dr. Fielding asked. "I'll be out in the Jeep if you need me. If you see anything suspicious, radio me straight away on my walkie-talkie."

Ulf gently picked Tiana up and headed outside. He placed her in a patch of sunshine at the foot of the observatory tower.

"Wait here a moment," he said. "I just need to get something."

Ulf raced to his den and came back clutching *The Book of Beasts*.

"What's that for?" Tiana asked.

"I'll show you," Ulf said, opening the door to the tower. He carried Tiana up the spiral staircase to the observatory at the top of Farraway Hall.

Chapter 17

AT THE BOTTOM OF A PIT IN FURNACE WOODS, the big man Bone was leaning on a sledgehammer, wiping the sweat from his forehead. "Finished," he called up.

The small man Blud was looking down, wiping his nose with a red rag. "Is it secure?" he asked.

Poking from the ground next to Bone's foot was a huge metal ring. Bone kicked it, making sure it was firmly fastened. "That dragon won't be going any-where once she's chained down."

With the sledgehammer over his shoulder, Bone climbed the tall ladder up the pit wall. All around the top of the pit, wooden stakes were sticking out like spears. The big man clambered between them and pulled the ladder up. He stood on the edge of the pit, admiring his work.

"The Baron will be pleased," Blud said.

"What else is he getting?" Bone asked. "The dragon can't fight itself."

Blud stuffed the red rag into his pocket. "Something from the RSPCB," he said, sniggering.

Just then, they heard the sound of a truck in the distance. It was coming through the woods.

"Quick, hide!" Blud said.

Blud and Bone grabbed their tools and the ladder and ran into the bushes.

A large black truck drove into the clearing. It stopped, and Inspector Black jumped down from the driver's seat. "We're here, Mr. Orson," he said, opening the back doors.

The giant squeezed out of the truck and saw the pit.

"Blimey," Orson said. He stepped over to the edge and looked down. "That's a Ring of Horrors, all right. Those stakes will stop anything escaping."

"It looks like someone's been here recently," the Inspector told him, examining a footprint in the mud at the edge of the pit. "Get the apples, ropes, and chains, Mr. Orson. They could be back any minute."

While Inspector Black examined the footprints, Orson unloaded everything from the back of the truck.

"What do you want me to do with all this?" Orson asked.

"Rescue the beast, of course. The ropes and chains are to secure the dragon. The apples, Mr. Orson, are for you—in case you get hungry. I need you to stay here and keep watch."

"What are you going to do?"

From inside his coat, Inspector Black pulled out the bundle of papers that Dr. Fielding had given him.

"I'm going to check out these criminals."

He got back into his truck. "Remember. Stay alert in case the beast hunter comes." He started the engine. "We'll catch him, Mr. Orson."

Inspector Black gave a thumbs–up, then drove the truck out of the clearing.

"Right you are," Orson called after him.

The giant placed the kit and the barrels at the edge of the clearing, then paced around the pit. He stepped slowly, glancing from side to side, looking out for criminals or dragons. The clearing was surrounded by tall trees. He peered through the branches into the shadows.

Around and around he went. And each time he circled the pit, he looked across at the two barrels and sniffed. He could smell the apples.

He stepped over to a barrel, reached in, and took out two handfuls of apples, then popped them into his mouth. They tasted delicious.

He glanced around at the bushes and trees.

There was no sign of anyone.

The woods were quiet.

It was tough keeping watch. There weren't any beasts to rescue. In fact, there wasn't really very much at all to do. Except eat.

Orson sat down on the ground with the two barrels on either side of him. He dug in, eating handful after handful of apples. They tasted sweet and juicy.

He scarfed two or three at a time, apple juice running down his chin.

"Mmmm, lovely apples," he muttered.

In no time at all, the barrels were empty and the giant's belly was full.

Orson leaned against a tree and stretched out his legs. As he kept watch, his eyes began to feel heavy.

He yawned. Soon he was snoring.

Just then, in the bushes, something moved.

Blud crept out wearing a gas mask. On his back was a cylinder of tranquilizer gas. While Orson snored, Blud pointed the tube under the giant's nose and sprayed the gas.

The giant slumped to the ground.

Blud pulled off the gas mask. "Tie him up!" he called.

Bone stepped out from the bushes and picked up the ropes and chains beside Orson. He started wrapping them tightly around the giant's legs. He wrapped Orson's arms and tied his hands behind his back, locking them with the padlock.

Blud ran off through the trees as Bone wrapped the rope around the giant's head, gagging his mouth.

There was the sound of an engine as a yellow crane trundled noisily into the clearing. Its caterpillar tracks squashed the bushes and trees in its path. Blud was sitting in the cab pulling levers. Attached to the arm of the crane was a long steel cable with a hook on its end. The crane belched smoke as Blud swung its arm above Orson.

Bone steadied the hook. As the hook lowered, he

attached it to the ropes and chains around Orson's ankles.

"Up you go," Bone said.

Blud pulled the levers in the crane, and Orson lifted up off the ground, hanging upside down. He was as tall as the trees, swinging from side to side, and fast asleep.

"Let's get out of here," Bone called. He climbed up to the back of the cab behind Blud, and the crane drove into the woods, taking Orson with it.

Chapter 18

UP IN THE OBSERVATORY, ULF WAS FLICKING through *The Book of Beasts*. Tiana was sitting on the table by the window.

"Here we are," Ulf said. "How to treat a fairy's sparkle." He showed Tiana the page.

Tiana looked at the words. "They're all blurry," she said.

Ulf read them to her: "If a fairy has lost its sparkle, it needs something sweet: a drop of honey, a blackberry, or a pinch of sugar."

Ulf walked to the kettle in the corner of the room where Dr. Fielding made her tea. Next to the kettle was an RSPCB mug and a bowl of sugar cubes.

He picked up a sugar cube and gave it to Tiana. "Here you are," he said. "Eat this."

The fairy held the sugar cube in her arms and licked it. "Thank you," she said weakly.

Ulf stepped over to the window. He looked out over the beast park to Troll Crag, the biodomes, and the aviary. The Roc was still lying on the ground.

"What did the book say about the Roc?" Ulf asked.

"It needs an orchid," Tiana told him. "There are some in the forest."

Ulf saw Dr. Fielding driving her Jeep across the marsh, heading for the seawater lagoon. Sunset Mountain looked still and quiet, casting a shadow over the Great Grazing Grounds. The big beasts were feeding in their enclosures.

Ulf scanned the perimeter fence from the hills to the ocean. "No sign of any intruders," he said.

Tiana didn't reply. She was busy licking the sugar cube.

Ulf looked across the room to the map on the wall. "Inspector Black said Marackai was a place in Africa."

Tiana sat up, half a wet sugar cube in her arms. "I don't like Inspector Black," she said. "He's not nice at all."

The color was slowly coming back into her cheeks.

Ulf went to the big map on the wall and looked for Africa.

"Africa's miles away from here," he said. He looked for the word *Marackai*. "Madagascar, Mali, Morocco, Mozambique, Malawi, Mombassa…" There was no Marackai anywhere.

"Marackai!" Tiana shouted.

Ulf looked over.

Tiana was flapping her wings, trying to lift herself off the table. "Marackai! Look!"

Ulf ran to her.

She was sitting on the word Marackai. Ulf lifted her up.

Underneath her, on the table, was the newspaper clipping with the photograph of a man and boy watching a small dragon taking off from a garden lawn:

PROFESSOR FARRAWAY'S DRAGON

Next to the photo, Ulf read: "Lord Farraway, Professor of cryptozoology, and his son Marackai Farraway, releasing the RSPCB's first dragon, Aziza."

Ulf looked at the photograph. "Marackai is the Professor's son!" he said.

"The boy?" Tiana asked.

"This photo was taken years ago. He'd be much older now."

Just then, Ulf heard a tapping sound on the

window. He looked up. Outside, Druce was hanging upside down, his nose pressed to the glass.

"Hello, Druce," Tiana said.

The gargoyle put his finger to his lips. "Ssshhh," he said.

"What do you want, Druce?" Ulf asked.

"Marrrrraaack-k-kai," the gargoyle gurgled. "Wick-edest boy you ever saw. Face like a rotten apple core."

Druce pointed at the newspaper clipping. Ulf looked closely at the photograph. The Professor's son was scowling. His face was screwed up and twisted.

Druce slid open the window and leaned in. "He kills beasts just for fun. Prods and pokes them till he's done."

The boy in the photgraph was holding a stick. He was poking it at the dragon. The end had been sharpened to a point.

"Look at his hand," Tiana said. The boy's little finger was missing.

Druce sucked on his finger, making a popping sound. "I bited him," he said, grinning.

"You bit his finger off?" Ulf asked. "You bit Marackai?"

Druce giggled. "Nasty Marackai. Went away, he did. Good riddance."

"He's back," Ulf said to Tiana. "Marackai Farraway's got the dragon."

"Ssshhh," Druce said. The gargoyle's ears pricked up. He scuttled onto the observatory roof and stared up the driveway. He stuck out his tongue, then turned to stone.

Ulf heard an engine. He rushed to the north window. Inspector Black was driving down the driveway in his black truck.

Ulf grabbed the walkie-talkie from the table. He turned it on.

"Dr. Fielding!" he said. "Dr. Fielding! They're back!"

The sun was starting to go down behind Sunset

Mountain. Dr. Fielding was driving the Jeep through the yard to the courtyard.

Ulf watched as she pulled up and stepped out to let the Inspector through the front gates. She reached into her white coat and took out her walkie-talkie. Ulf heard a hiss and then a crackle, and then Dr. Fielding's voice: "Hello, Ulf. Good news. Inspector Black has captured the criminal. Orson has saved the dragon."

Chapter 19

ULF GAVE TIANA THE WALKIE-TALKIE AND
another sugar cube. She wasn't strong enough to fly
yet. She waited by the window as Ulf bounded down
the spiral stairs.

He ran to the courtyard. Dr. Fielding and Inspector
Black were standing by the RSPCB helicopter.

"We should take the beast cradle, in case we have
to bring the dragon back here," Dr. Fielding said. She
had her medical bag in one hand and her pilot's
goggles in the other.

"What's happening?" Ulf asked.

"Good news," Inspector Black said. He stood with

his hands on his hips looking very pleased with himself. "At this very moment, Orson has the criminal tied up in Furnace Woods."

"I know who he is! It's Marackai Farraway," Ulf said.

The Inspector's eye twitched. "What are you talking about?" he asked.

Ulf looked at Dr. Fielding. "Marackai Farraway is the beast hunter! He's Professor Farraway's son."

The Inspector took hold of Dr. Fielding's arm. "Dr. Fielding, we should hurry. We need to go before it gets dark."

"But—" Ulf tried to stop her.

"I won't be long, Ulf," Dr. Fielding said. "I've just got to check that the dragon's okay. I'll be back in time for your transformation."

Dr. Fielding opened the door of the helicopter and put her medical bag inside. "Ulf, please would you be helpful and fetch the beast cradle for me? It's in the kit room."

"Come on, werewolf, I'll help you," Inspector Black said. The Inspector took Ulf by the hand and walked him toward the yard.

"It's all right. I can do it myself," Ulf said.

The Inspector gripped Ulf's hand tightly. He smiled and looked around. "Marvelous place you have here, isn't it?" he said. "Fresh air. Lovely views."

Inspector Black's leather glove felt cold against Ulf's hairy palm.

"You must love growing up here. Mountains, lake, sea—you really have it all."

They walked past the kit room.

"Where are we going?" Ulf asked. "The beast cradle's in there."

"You even have your own little den," Inspector Black said.

He dragged Ulf out of the yard, walking him along the paddock fence. The door to Ulf's den was open.

"Ah, look, Dr. Fielding's given you lovely fresh straw."

Ulf tried to pull his hand away.

"In you go!" the Inspector said, pushing Ulf inside. Inspector Black slammed the door and turned the key in the lock. "Werewolves shouldn't be allowed out on the night of a full moon," he said.

He pulled the key out and threw it into the paddock.

Ulf rattled the bars.

"Dr. Fielding!" he called. "Dr. Fielding!"

"Dr. Fielding can't hear you," Inspector Black said.

Ulf heard the sound of the helicopter's engine starting up in the courtyard.

"She and I are going on a little . . . expedition," the Inspector said.

He put his hand through the bars of the cage and stroked Ulf's head.

Ulf tried to step back but the Inspector gripped his hair.

"Such lovely thick hair. You'd make a good rug."

Ulf bit the Inspector's hand.

"Ow!"

The Inspector's glove came off.

Ulf stared.

The Inspector's little finger was missing.

"You're not an inspector at all!" Ulf yelled. "You're Marackai Farraway!"

"That's *Baron* Marackai to you." He smiled. A wide grin stretched across his face to his ears.

He threw his head back and started laughing. "Ha ha haaaa ha haa ha haaaa ha ha haaaa!"

As he laughed, his grin didn't move. Even when he stopped laughing, it was still stretched wide across his face.

It was stuck.

He pressed his fingers to his cheeks, pushing the corners of his mouth back into place. Then he took his hat off and dug his fingers into the skin on his neck. It was rubber, like a mask.

He pulled it up, and underneath, Ulf saw a face

that was old and twisted with hatred like a rotten apple core.

He leaned toward Ulf. "I've been away. But now I'm back."

He was scowling. It was the same scowl Ulf had seen on the boy in the photograph. His eye twitched. "My father was crazy to leave this place to beasts. It should have been mine."

Ulf leaped at him, bouncing off the bars. "You shot the baby dragon! You've kidnapped Aziza!"

Marackai smiled, rolling his rubber mask back down, and slipped his glove back on.

"Where's Orson? What have you done with Orson?"

"I'd love to stop and chat," he said. "But I have to go to Furnace Woods. I have a Ring of Horrors to attend. Dr. Fielding's in for quite a surprise."

He hurried off toward the courtyard. "I'll be back for you later," he called.

Ulf furiously rattled the bars. "Dr. Fielding! Tiana! Druce!"

He could hear the helicopter blades starting to turn.

"Help! Somebody help!"

Ulf looked up at the house. Druce was on the rooftop, as still as stone.

"Tiana!" Ulf called.

A sparkle came flying from the observatory window. It sputtered through the air, dipping and weaving.

"I'm coming," her tiny voice called. Her sparkle was fizzing weakly. She fell down at Ulf's door.

"Let me out, Tiana!" Ulf said. "Inspector Black is Marackai Farraway. He's tricked us!"

"Where's the key?" Tiana asked.

"He threw it into the paddock."

Tiana flew off to find it. "I can't see it," she said, flying low over the grass.

From the courtyard, Ulf could hear the *thwock thwock thwock* of the helicopter blades.

"Hurry up!" he called. "They're about to take off. He's got Dr. Fielding!"

"Found it!" Tiana called, dragging the key across the grass to Ulf's den.

Ulf picked it up and unlocked the door. "We have to stop them!" he said.

Ulf leaped out of his den and raced toward the front of the house.

"Stop, Dr. Fielding!" he shouted.

But he was too late. The helicopter was rising above Farraway Hall. Ulf stood in the yard and watched as it banked, heading northward. He saw it getting smaller and smaller as it flew into the distance.

Tiana hovered beside him.

"Dr. Fielding's in danger!" Ulf said.

"Then you have to go after her."

"But how?" Ulf asked.

"You'll have to fly," Tiana told him. "Meet me by the Roc!"

Chapter 20

TIANA SHOT OFF ACROSS THE PADDOCK TO the Dark Forest, a trail of sparkles sputtering behind her.

Ulf ran along the track to the aviary. He sprinted through the mesh tunnel, past the griffin and the vampire owls, and out the other end.

The Roc was lying on the ground. It looked up at Ulf with big sad eyes.

"Don't worry," Ulf said to it. "Tiana's got a surprise for you."

The Roc screeched.

Tiana came flying from the Dark Forest. "Look

what I've got," she called. In her arms, she was carrying a flower with white petals. "It's an orchid," she said.

Tiana laid the flower on the ground in front of the Roc. "It's time to go home," she said.

The Roc leaned forward and sniffed the flower, then started cooing happily.

"It's working!" Ulf said. The Roc's big yellow eyes blinked.

"It likes it," Tiana said.

Ulf stroked the Roc's head with his hairy hand. The Roc looked up at the sky. It stood up and shook its feathers.

"Can I have a ride?" Ulf asked it.

The beast lowered its head to the ground. Ulf took hold of the golden feathers on the Roc's neck and pulled himself up. He sat on its back, gripping its feathers with both hands. "Let's go," he said.

The Roc beat its wings and lunged into the air. It took off, flying upward into the evening sky.

Ulf looked down.

"Wait for me!" Tiana called. She frantically flut-tered her wings and, in a burst of sparkles, shot up and tumbled onto the Roc's back, landing in its feathers.

The Roc flew high above the biodomes, soaring over Sunset Mountain. Ulf looked out over the land and sea, the wind blowing through his hair. The air tasted clean and cold. The sun was setting, and the clouds glowed red.

"Which way's Furnace Woods?" Ulf asked.

"North," Tiana said, whispering into the Roc's ear.

The Roc banked in a wide circle.

"Full speed ahead!" Ulf said.

The Roc swooped down over the Great Grazing Grounds and the Dark Forest, clipping the treetops. The bulltoxic bellowed from the paddock.

As the Roc soared over Farraway Hall, Ulf looked down on the chimneys and the rooftop. Druce the gargoyle was dancing and waving. "Go, Fur Face," he called.

The Roc flew over the perimeter fence, and Ulf looked at the fields in the far distance. He had never seen them before.

"Keep an eye out for the helicopter," Tiana said.

Ulf sat up to look over the top of the Roc's head, and the cold wind hit him full in the face. The light was fading, and there was no sign of the helicopter in the sky ahead. "They'll be miles away by now," he said.

The Roc beat its wings, gathering speed. Ulf wobbled. He leaned forward, flattening himself against the Roc's neck.

"Try to relax," Tiana said. "It won't let you fall."

The Roc screeched, and Ulf slowly let his grip loosen on its feathers. They sped over moorland and fields of sheep. Looking westward, Ulf could see the blood-red sun sinking below the horizon. The sky was growing darker. He could feel the hairs tingling on his hands.

"Look, Ulf!" Tiana said, pointing down. "Houses."
Ahead on the ground, tiny yellow lights dotted a valley.

Ulf looked to the East. The clouds were parting. From behind them the full moon appeared.

Ulf saw it, and his eyes flashed silver.

He felt the bones in his chest cracking.

His transformation had begun.

Chapter 21

A STRONG, SHARP PAIN BURST IN THE BACK OF Ulf's neck. He drew his knees up under him, trying not to let go of the Roc's feathers.

He could feel his backbone bending and his chest cracking. In the moonlight, his skeleton was realigning. His skin stretched. He could feel his muscles tightening and growing, ripping his T-shirt and tearing his jeans.

He gripped tightly. The hair on the back of his hands started spreading. His nails lengthened, turning into claws. His tail was emerging and thick dark hair was growing over his whole body.

Fangs split through his gums, pushing his lips open. He felt his tongue lengthening, dripping with saliva. His lower jaw thrust forward and his whole face twisted into that of a wolf.

Ulf looked up at the full moon. He threw his head back and howled.

With wolf eyes he could see further. He could hear every sound. Smells were filling his nostrils.

In the distance, the landscape darkened. He could see a vast blanket of trees.

"That's Furnace Woods," Tiana said.

As the Roc thundered onward, Ulf sniffed the air. He could smell the scent of humans. He glanced down as the Roc shot over the tops of tall pine trees. They flashed below in a blur.

Up ahead, Ulf saw a circle of bright lights. His ears pricked up. He could hear humans cheering.

A man was speaking through a megaphone. "Ladies and Gentlemen, welcome to the Ring of Horrors!"

In the shadows, Ulf could make out a crowd of humans.

They were gathered beside a huge round pit dug into the ground. They were waving money and shaking their fists.

On either side of the pit, the tall arms of two cranes were poking from the treetops. As the Roc swooped lower, Ulf looked down.

He saw Dr. Fielding, gagged and tied to a post. Next to her, standing on a mound of earth, was a man dressed in a fur coat. His face was twisted and rotten.

Tiana gasped. "Who's that?" she asked.

Ulf bared his fangs and snarled: "That's Marackai!"

Baron Marackai waved, then held a megaphone to his lips. "I, Baron Marackai, welcome you to an historic night."

The crowd cheered.

The Roc swooped lower, circling.

"I would like to thank our special guest, Dr.

Helen Fielding, for helping me gather you all together."

Ulf saw Franco Ravioli the chef, Lucretia Da Silva the boutique manager, and Billy Buck the factory owner. Baron Marackai had invited all the criminals from Dr. Fielding's files!

"For too long, the RSPCB has meddled in our world," Baron Marackai said. "Now it's their turn to suffer. The RSPCB is over! The beasts shall soon be ours!"

The Baron removed his gloves and raised his right hand. "Death to the RSPCB!"

All the humans in the crowd folded down their little fingers and held up their right hands.

"Death to the RSPCB!" they cheered. They began chanting: "Ba-ron, Ba-ron, Ba-ron, Ba-ron."

"And so to the main event," Baron Marackai said. "For your entertainment I give you a fight between two heavyweights. The first, a fire breather!"

From out of the trees a crane trundled to the

edge of the pit. Swinging from the crane's arm on a steel wire was a huge metal cage draped in a tarpaulin. It was rocking and clattering.

A big man with a thick beard and long greasy hair stepped out of the crane's cabin and climbed down a ladder into the pit. Hanging from the bars of the cage was a chain. The big man attached the chain to a metal ring at the bottom of the pit and climbed back out.

"Ladies and Gentlemen," the Baron announced. "I give you Aziza, the firebelly dragon!" The doors of the cage burst open, and Aziza the dragon tumbled out screeching into the Ring of Horrors.

The dragon stood in the pit beating her wings. She tried to take off but she couldn't. She was tied to the ground, the chain attached to a metal collar on her neck. Her back legs were tied together with another chain so she couldn't run.

The dragon roared, and a jet of flames shot out of the pit.

"Facing Aziza, we have a beast with the strength of a hundred men."

The crowd parted as a second crane trundled to the edge of the pit.

"Here for the first and possibly last time, our challenger—the RSPCB's very own giant!"

Hanging upside down from the crane's steel wire was Orson. The crane jerked, and the wire slackened.

Orson fell crashing into the pit.

Chapter 22

FROM THE BACK OF THE ROC, ULF COULD SEE Orson standing in the Ring of Horrors. The giant's clothes were torn and dirty. His face was covered in mud. His feet were tied with chains.

The crowd booed and hissed.

Aziza the dragon lurched forward, roaring at the giant.

"Fight!" Baron Marackai shouted.

"Fight! Fight! Fight!" the crowd chanted.

"We have to save Orson!" Ulf growled, looking down. "How do you land this beast?"

Tiana whispered into the Roc's ear, then leaped off.

"Tiana!" Ulf roared. "Wait for me!"

Tiana flew down toward the pit as the Roc carried Ulf away.

At the bottom of the pit, Orson faced the dragon.

"Whoa there," he said, holding his hands out. "There's a good dragon. Easy girl."

The dragon clawed the ground. Steam was pouring from her nostrils. She looked up and let out a series of short, high-pitched screeches, calling for her baby.

"Your baby's gone," Orson said to her. "It's dead."

Baron Marackai reached into the pit with a long, sharp pole and jabbed the dragon in the eye. Aziza the dragon roared, baring teeth as sharp as knives. She thrashed her tail, snapping the pole into pieces.

As her tail whipped around, Orson tried to jump out of the way. The chains around his ankles tightened, and he stumbled and fell.

The dragon saw him and beat her wings. A jet of fire erupted from her mouth.

Orson crouched in the dirt, burying his head in his arms. The dragon's fire engulfed him. The crowd cheered.

"Stop it!" Tiana yelled. Her tiny voice was drowned out by the cheering. She flew into the pit, and the dragon spewed another jet of fire, forcing her back.

Orson rolled out of the way, crashing against the dirt wall. He jumped up and threw himself at the dragon, wrapping his arms around her neck. Aziza was raging, shaking her head, trying to bite Orson. The giant pressed his shoulder into her side, holding on with his massive arms. Aziza's legs started to buckle. Orson heaved, trying to pull her to the ground.

Just then, the dragon's tail whipped around, smashing against Orson's head.

Orson clung on. "I'm not going to hurt you," he said, trying to calm her.

The Baron reached in with a pole, jabbing Orson in the neck. "Ow!" Orson said, letting go.

The dragon lashed with her tail. It smashed Orson's jaw, knocking him backward. He tripped on his chains, crashing to the floor of the pit. The back of his head hit the metal ring poking from the ground.

Orson lay still. His eyes were closed.

"Orson!" Tiana cried.

The dragon stood over him, red-hot spit dripping from her mouth.

"Kill!" Baron Marackai shouted.

"Kill! Kill! Kill! Kill! Kill!" the crowd chanted.

Just then a long, loud howl sounded from the woods. It echoed around the clearing.

The chanting stopped.

The crowd gasped as a werewolf leaped from the trees and jumped into the Ring of Horrors.

Chapter 23

"WEREWOLF!" BARON MARACKAI HISSED.

Ulf crouched between Orson and the dragon, baring his fangs. He could smell blood, sweat, and fire.

"You're going to die, werewolf!" Baron Marackai shouted. He held up his megaphone. "Ladies and gentlemen. This beast wants to die!"

The crowd cheered.

"For your pleasure and delight, I give you werewolf versus dragon!"

Ulf looked up and saw humans cheering, waving their fists.

"Werewolf versus dragon. Werewolf versus dragon. Werewolf versus dragon," they chanted.

Ulf saw Dr. Fielding desperately trying to free herself from the ropes.

Ulf faced the dragon.

He could smell her fiery breath. He looked into the dragon's eyes. Inside they were burning and swirling with rage.

Aziza screeched, smoke pouring from her nostrils. Then she lunged, her mouth wide open, exposing rows of razor-sharp teeth.

Ulf jumped backward.

The dragon lunged again, and Ulf leaped up the side of the pit.

He dug his claws into the earth and ran around the pit wall, dragon fire licking at his heels, singeing his fur.

Aziza twisted and turned.

Ulf leaped off the wall onto the dragon's tail. He scrambled up her hard scaly back and clung on, hooking his claws into the metal collar around the dragon's neck. It was wet with blood.

The dragon tried to turn and bite Ulf. She was roaring, throwing her head one way, then the other.

Baron Marackai threw a rock, and it hit Ulf on the shoulder. Ulf's grip loosened, and he fell crashing to the floor of the pit.

The dragon came for him with her claws outstretched. The crowd cheered, shouting for more: "Kill him! Kill him! Kill the werewolf!"

Ulf rolled to the side as the dragon's claws raked the ground, gouging out clumps of earth and stones.

The dragon lunged, her jaws wide open. Ulf threw himself out of the way just in time to see the dragon's teeth slam into the ground.

Ulf sprang to his feet. He ran underneath the dragon's belly, diving at the chain between her legs.

He bit straight through the metal.

The chain snapped and the dragon's foot stamped down, just missing Ulf's head.

"The werewolf's crazy!" someone shouted from the crowd.

Ulf bounded from underneath the dragon's belly, and the dragon twisted around, trying to tear him to pieces.

Her tail was lashing. Ulf leaped onto it, hooking his claws into the scales, clinging on for his life. He clawed his way onto the dragon's back and desperately held on as the dragon started bucking, trying to throw him off.

Ulf pulled himself along the dragon's neck and Baron Marackai hurled another rock. "Die, were-wolf!"

The rock missed and struck Aziza in the eye. She looked up.

Ulf growled: "It was him. He killed your baby."

Ulf bit through the chain on her metal collar. The chain snapped. Aziza the dragon shook her neck, and the chain fell to the ground. "You're free," Ulf growled.

"You fool!" the Baron shouted. "You stupid werewolf!"

Ulf dropped down off Aziza's back and stood on all fours, panting. He looked up to see the dragon opening her mouth. He braced himself for more flames.

Instead, he felt Aziza's hot breath warm his fur. She was panting too. She turned her head and looked up at the Baron on the edge of the pit.

Aziza roared. Ulf howled. The crowd began screaming. Ulf could smell their fear.

The dragon beat her wings, and Ulf gripped on to her tail as she rose out of the pit. He jumped off, landing on all fours in front of the humans.

The dragon took off into the air, and the crowd began running, fleeing the clearing. Aziza swooped after them, scorching the ground with her fire.

The humans ran away as fast as they could into the woods.

The small man in the ragged suit and the big man

with the thick beard leaped into the cranes. They drove off through the trees.

As they fled, the Baron was shouting, "Cowards! Come back, Blud! Come back, Bone!"

Baron Marackai threw down his megaphone and picked up a rifle. He took aim and fired at the dragon. The bullet shot across the clearing and ricocheted off the dragon's hard scales. Ulf watched as Aziza hovered in the air beating her wings, screeching at the Baron.

Baron Marackai took aim, shooting again and again.

Aziza blasted a jet of fire.

"Not my face!" the Baron screamed. He tried to shield his face as the flames engulfed him. His fur coat was burning. He furiously patted the flames, trying to put them out. Smoke was rising off him.

Ulf saw Aziza soaring away into the night sky. He looked back at the Baron's sooty face. It was clenched with anger.

"You horrible, useless, little piece of fur," the

Baron spat. He loaded a shiny bullet into his rifle and pointed it at Ulf. "You can be the first to die."

Ulf snarled.

"Leave him alone!" a shrill voice shouted. It was Tiana. She flew between Ulf and the Baron.

"Don't worry, fairy, you're next," Baron Marackai said. He cocked the trigger. "Say bye-bye, werewolf. The RSPCB won't save you now."

He was about to pull the trigger when a shadow loomed overhead.

He looked up. "Noooo!" he cried.

It was the dragon. A set of huge claws reached down from the sky, plucking the Baron from the ground. As the claws grabbed him, he dropped the rifle.

"Get off me!" Baron Marackai shouted. "Get off me!"

Ulf watched as Aziza beat her wings and rose into the air with Baron Marackai dangling beneath her. He was kicking his legs.

Aziza the dragon was lifting the Baron high above the treetops into the sky. She screeched, carrying him off into the night.

"I'll be back!" Baron Marackai shouted. "You'll see!"

Ulf ran to Dr. Fielding and bit through the ropes around her arms and legs, releasing her.

She tore the gag from her mouth. "Ulf, are you okay?"

Ulf smiled with his fangs.

Then he heard a groan from the bottom of the pit and looked down. It was Orson. "Where's the dragon?" the giant asked. He was sitting up, rubbing his head.

"It's over, Orson," Dr. Fielding called down to him.

Ulf looked up and howled at the moon.

Chapter 24

THE NEXT DAY ULF WOKE UP IN HIS DEN. HIS wolf hair had disappeared back under his skin. The door to his den was open. Outside were a pair of jeans and a T-shirt. He slipped them on.

Tiana flew toward him, humming to herself.

"Ulf!" she said. "You're back!"

Ulf looked at his hands. They were filthy. He had just a patch of hair on each palm, and his claws had gone.

He looked out at the sky. It was a bright sunny day. It would be a whole month until the next full moon.

"Dr. Fielding let you stay out all night," Tiana told him.

"In the wild?" Ulf asked.

"Don't you remember?"

Ulf licked his teeth. His fangs were gone.

"Not really," he told her.

"You're a hero," Tiana said.

Ulf heard a trumpeting roar. He looked over and saw Orson leading the biganasty out of the Big Beast Barn.

"Orson!" he called.

The giant waved. "Thank you, Ulf!"

"You saved his life," Tiana said, hovering outside Ulf's den. She smiled, then shot off in a burst of sparkles, following Orson across the paddock to the Dark Forest.

Ulf found Dr. Fielding in her office. She was writing.

"Is everything all right?" Ulf asked her.

"Everything's fine, Ulf. Thanks to you."

Dr. Fielding put down her pen and slipped a piece of paper into a file labeled BARON MARACKAI. She stamped the file with a rubber stamp: CASE SOLVED.

The Helping Hand crawled out from the storeroom.

"Will you file this, please?" Dr. Fielding said to it.

The Helping Hand picked the file up and scuttled off.

"Marackai would have tricked us all if it hadn't been for you, Ulf."

"He locked me up," Ulf told her. "He said he'd come back to take what was his."

"Nothing is his," Dr. Fielding said. She took a piece of paper from her desk and showed it to Ulf. It read:

The Last Will and Testament of
Lord John Everard Farraway

"This is Professor Farraway's will," Dr. Fielding said. "Marackai was nineteen years old when the Professor died. The Professor left everything he had to the RSPCB. Marackai got nothing."

Ulf looked at the will. It was old and dusty. He thought about the ghost in the library and how it had tried to warn him.

"Marackai was nasty," Ulf told her. "Druce says he was cruel to beasts."

"Marackai must have wanted Farraway Hall for himself," Dr. Fielding said. "He seems to have been planning his return extremely carefully. He must have known all about the dragon migration, and realized that NICE wouldn't send an inspector straightaway."

Dr. Fielding stood up and went to the window.

Outside, a shiny black car was pulling up at the entrance gates.

"About time," Dr. Fielding said.

"Who's that?" Ulf asked, following her to the courtyard.

Ulf watched as a man stepped out of the car. He was short and fat, dressed in a black coat and a bowler hat.

"My name's Inspector Hector," he said. "I'm from NICE. I'm very sorry I'm so late. I've come about the dragon."

"Then you'd better come inside. You can park next to that truck," Dr. Fielding said.

She pointed to the Baron's big black truck in the courtyard. "We have much to discuss."

While Dr. Fielding led Inspector Hector to her office, Ulf headed to the tower. He ran up the spiral stairs to the observatory and grabbed *The Book of Beasts* from the table where he'd left it.

He looked out of the window at the beast park. He looked toward the aviary. The Roc would be back home by now, he thought.

Ulf heard a tapping sound and looked up. Druce

the gargoyle was dancing on the glass dome. He started singing: "He kills beasts just for fun. But not this time, cuz Fur Face won!"

The gargoyle blew a loud raspberry at Ulf, then scuttled back along the rooftop to his perch.

Ulf headed down the spiral staircase with *The Book of Beasts*.

Halfway down, in the wall of the tower, he opened a door that led into the main house. He stepped into a dusty room with a grand piano. A giant moth was hanging from the ceiling, and wood lice the size of cats scurried across the floor.

Ulf hurried through the room and out into the Gallery of Science. He ran the full length of the corridor, through the Room of Curiosities to the door of the library. The door creaked open, and Ulf stepped into the darkness.

He felt his way to the painting. "Professor Farraway? Are you here?"

A candle flickered on.

"It's over. Marackai's gone," Ulf said.

Ulf placed *The Book of Beasts* on the table beside the candle. "Thank you for the book, Professor," he said.

As he turned to leave, he heard a noise behind him. He looked back and saw the book floating toward him. It pushed itself into his hand.

Ulf turned it over. On the back, written in dust, were the words:

THIS BOOK WILL SAVE YOUR LIFE.

"But we're safe now, Professor," he said. "Aren't we?"

Ulf felt an icy draft pass straight through him, and the candle blew out.

The end . . .for now